THE DRIEST SEASON

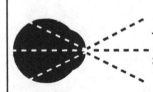

This Large Print Book carries the
Seal of Approval of N.A.V.H.

THE DRIEST SEASON

MEGHAN KENNY

THORNDIKE PRESS
A part of Gale, a Cengage Company

GALE
A Cengage Company

Farmington Hills, Mich • San Francisco • New York • Waterville, Maine
Meriden, Conn • Mason, Ohio • Chicago

LIBRARY OF CONGRESS CIP DATA ON FILE.
CATALOGUING IN PUBLICATION FOR THIS BOOK
IS AVAILABLE FROM THE LIBRARY OF CONGRESS

ISBN-13: 978-1-4328-5014-2 (hardcover)

Published in 2018 by arrangement with W.W. Norton & Company, Inc.

Printed in Mexico
1 2 3 4 5 6 7 22 21 20 19 18

For my grandmother,
Wilma Lucile Jacobson Bredahl,
1918–2011

HOW LONG DID YOU SLEEP?

Dare you do this —
open your eyes
and look around?
Yes, you're here,
here in this world,
you're not dreaming,
it's just as
you see it, things here
are like this.
Like this?
Yes, just like this,
not otherwise.
How long did you sleep?

— Olav H. Hague

CHAPTER ONE

In that driest season, Cielle's father hanged himself in the barn. A rope tied to a beam above stacked bales of hay, a wheelbarrow, rusted cans. Cielle found him. Home from summer school in the middle of July, and her legs couldn't move beneath her. She looked and didn't look. Her father hung still, bloated and blue. She thought of chickens, pigs, and hides of cows tied up and heavy-looking on ropes and hooks at the butcher's.

Cielle wasn't a child, nearly sixteen. She walked closer and touched his boot. Jesus. Sweet Jesus. She knelt before her father and thought for a moment he could fall. Light came in from rafter windows and cut long square shadows on wood plank walls. Then light shifted to dark from what she knew to be passing clouds. The barn was cool and damp. Sharp pebbles dug at her knees. She didn't look at his face again, or his hands, or all that was him outside of his clothing. Because it wasn't him right there, but something else, someone unrecognizable, and a memory she didn't want. Why had she gone into the barn? She never went in first thing after school. But that day she did and she couldn't remember the reason.

Their farm wasn't large, but it paid. It was a living. Wheat, corn, hay, oats, alfalfa, tobacco, chickens, pigs, and dairy cows. Their house was two hundred feet from the barn. Where was her mother? Helen, her sister, had gone to the lake. Cielle stood and touched his boot again. It floated above her shoulder.

"Daddy," she whispered.

She kept her eyes down and went to the house. The dirt road was dry and soft like flour. The red pickup truck was parked in front, and fresh garden radishes sat in a strainer in the kitchen sink. A pitcher of iced tea sat on the Formica table. She called for her mother, but there was no answer. She went out back into the garden, but no one was there. A breeze came through and rustled leaves. Cielle stood a moment at the door, expecting the world to stand still with her, but it didn't. Clouds like stretched gauze moved quickly above, the tire swing in the oak tree shifted, and its chains creaked.

She walked to the front yard. No one. But on the floor of the front porch, in neat order, was her father's wallet, his hat, a picture of her mother, of Helen, of herself, and of a young boy. On top of each photo was a heart-shaped stone. Stones they'd collected together at the lake. Their heart stones. Their hearts. She assumed the boy to be her father as a child, during a happier time. A time he wished he could go back to, before migraines. There was her family — lined up, paper on wood. The edges of the photos fluttered in the breeze.

Her father had headaches. Cielle knew dust and pollen made them worse every year and that doctors said there was nothing to do for them but wait out the season. "How does a farmer wait out a season?" her father would say. "Do they expect I sit in the house with a wet towel over my face?" He said it hurt to walk. Felt his head was caving in. He'd moan deep and low at night, as if there were something inside him trying to push up and out. He'd writhe on the bed, on the floor. He'd hit his forehead with his fists, hoping to jar and get rid of the pain. Once he asked Cielle to rub his temples, asked her if she felt anything out of the ordinary.

"Nothing," she said. "Just your regular head."

"My head is pulsing. It's pressure all over. How is a farmer allergic to everything, Cielle? That's the sorriest thing I ever heard."

Cielle went upstairs and laid her satchel on her bed. From her window she saw the barn: faded red paint and stone; tall and long; dark windows. She leaned down, put both hands on her bed, and shut her eyes. That morning before school she'd collected chicken eggs. She'd scrubbed them with a damp nailbrush by the coop behind the barn and rinsed them in hot bleach-water. She'd set up a chair and small table and laid the eggs on a towel to dry. Her father had said it might be time to cut for hay, and he walked the field. He stood far off — they had one hundred acres, some of it wooded, but mostly fields — and he seemed small in the tall alfalfa. She could make out his hands on his head, as if he were holding himself together.

He'd faced the woods and stood for some time, as if he were waiting for a sign of clouds or rain. They needed the water. After rain the air would clear and the allergies and headaches would be lessened or gone for days. Then her father turned toward her, the house, the barn. Cielle waved. He held his arm high, his hand wide open. Then he brought his hands to his mouth and a high-pitched, fluttery whistle reached her, distinct and clear. It was the birdcall he'd taught her. She'd asked him what he thought it meant, and he told her those birds were saying, *I'm right here. Find me.*

She heard noise in her mother's room. She walked the narrow hall, ran her hand along the beadboard wall. She kept slow and steady. If she moved any faster she'd trip over her own feet and fall face-first, heavy like a wooden door.

She found her mother in the claw-foot tub, lying still, looking at her feet in front of her; she did not bathe in the afternoon or during drought. Cielle sat on the rim and couldn't remember when she'd last seen her mother naked. Her arms and legs were tanned. Her stomach was white, rounded and swollen as if she were pregnant. Her nipples were wide brown circles.

"I found Daddy," Cielle said.

Her mother looked up at Cielle blankly, as if she couldn't quite locate her. She pulled her knees to her chest and lifted her right foot out of the water. The skin was white and shriveled. "Have you seen this blister on my foot? It doesn't want to go away."

"Mom, what should I do?"

"About this?" She rubbed her foot, and shook her head "There's nothing you can do."

"No, about Daddy in the barn." Cielle dipped her hand in the water and it was cold.

"He'll be back for dinner. Don't bother your father. We're just fine."

Cielle touched her mother's shoulder.

"Let me finish my bath," she said. "We'll be fine."

Cielle got in the truck and drove. It was a mile to the Mitchells' farm. She didn't want lights or noise or strangers taking her father away. The Mitchells were her parents' best friends. The road was graveled and straight. The steering wheel was big in her hands, and she sat far up on the seat to reach the pedals. Her armpits were damp, and her legs were sweaty and stuck to the vinyl. She held tight and drove fast. Waist-high corn divided into patterned rows, not as tall as usual for this time of year, and the stalks were yellowing, drying out in the heat. Irrigation wasn't enough without rainfall, and water was low all around. She knew from overheard conversations their farm was in trouble from the drought, but now this, now her father.

A small blue car came from the other direction and the driver slowed to wave. Her sister was in the car, heading for the house. Cielle pulled onto the shoulder and the blue car pulled over too, and Cielle stepped out of the truck and waited for Helen to walk to her. Helen wore a white eyelet dress and had braids. She was eighteen and tall, and her strides were slow and long. She was a beautiful girl.

"Where're you going?" Helen said.

"Mitchells'."

Helen waved off the car. It beeped and peeled out down the long stretch of road. Cielle watched it zoom away until it got so far it seemed to evaporate into the dust and heat waves just above the gravel. The girls got in the truck, Helen rolled down her window, and Cielle pulled back onto the road.

"What's wrong?" Helen said, and tapped her hand on her thigh.

Cielle looked straight ahead and shrugged. She put her hand to her mouth and bile inched up the back of her throat and the truck reached fifty-five, the fastest she had ever driven.

"Jesus, Cielle, slow down, the turn is coming." Helen put both hands on the dash.

Cielle turned left onto the bumpy dirt road to the Mitchells'. Bodie, eighteen and the only son and child, drove the tractor in the field, dust clouds billowing behind him. The diesel exhaust was dense in the humid air. He tipped his hat and waved. Helen knelt on the seat and leaned half out the window and whistled. Cielle pulled on her ankle, and she slid back down.

"I love him," Helen said, smiling, watching Bodie in her side-view mirror.

Cielle pulled up in front of the house. Bodie rode the tractor toward them. Helen went to meet him, and so Cielle knocked on the screen door and went inside. A fan ran on high and turned back and forth. It rippled her blouse like a wave, blew back her hair, and cooled her neck and arms. She breathed heavily, and her chest felt tight and thick, and she thought, *A long needle could be stuck right through me and I wouldn't feel a thing.*

Mrs. Mitchell walked into the kitchen with laundry in her arms, and laid it in a pile on the table.

"Cielle," she said, "you look hot. Some iced tea?"

Cielle nodded yes, and began folding bath towels.

"Leave that," Mrs. Mitchell said, and handed her a glass. She looked out the screen door and said, "You girls come for Bodie?"

Cielle wanted to say, *Daddy is dead,* but Bodie and Helen came in, chatting and flirty, their arms touching. *Nobody should have to know this,* she thought.

"I told Helen they could stay for supper," Bodie said to his mother. "That all right?"

"Of course," Mrs. Mitchell said, and patted her upper lip. "But I'm not baking anything, we'll just have beans and leftover chicken."

The cold drink felt good but Cielle felt light-headed, tired, as if she could lie down on the floor right then and sleep. She needed to tell someone about her father in the barn, her mother in the bath. But she knew to say the words out loud was to change lives instantly, and to throw the world off balance from that moment on. She remembered the barn swallows clucking and flapping high up in the rafters and her father's horse stomping in his stall. The sharp smell of urine. The wheelbarrow in which she'd carried the eggs that morning. Had he stood on it in his last moments? If she had put the wheelbarrow behind the barn, maybe none of this would have happened. Maybe if she'd done the birdcall back he would have known she loved him, but that morning her hands smelled of bleach and she didn't want them near her face, near her eyes. Now, at the Mitchells', all she could think of was the sharp smell of bleach on her fingers. Maybe if she didn't say the words *Daddy's dead,* didn't even think them and stayed at the Mitchells', then by the time they went home she would know it was imagined and her mother would be out of the bath in a cotton dress, and her father would be in for dinner. They would be sitting at the kitchen table eating steak and potatoes, listening to the ball game on the radio.

Mr. Mitchell walked in red-faced and sweaty. He wore a white undershirt tank and dirty pants held up by suspenders. He wiped his face on one of the folded towels and Mrs. Mitchell said, "Honest to God, Jim, not a good, clean towel."

Mr. Mitchell laughed. "Expect me to wipe my face with a dirty towel?"

"Just not a good bath towel," she said, and handed him a glass of iced tea, and he leaned in and kissed her on the cheek.

"I'll wash up for my sweetheart," he said,

and took a long drink, "just after Miss Cielle here might help me bring in a horse." He winked at Cielle, set his glass down, and held the door open for her.

The Mitchells owned two American quarter horse mares — compact, strong animals. They had English saddles and bridles and let Cielle ride when she wanted. Mrs. Mitchell gave lessons on weekends for extra money but taught Cielle for free.

Cielle walked behind Mr. Mitchell. His steps were heavy and sure in his work boots, and his soles left diamond patterns in the dirt. Cielle stretched her legs to step into his footprints as if they were tracks in the snow. She moved forward awkwardly like a circus clown with a wide, exaggerated walk. She saw him turn his head toward the pasture for the horses, but knew it was for a sideways glance of her behind him, and he smiled and continued on. He smelled like her father after work in the sun — musky and salty and alive.

He stopped at the barn to get halters and lead ropes, and Cielle waited outside for him. She heard him talk inside the barn, and then he came out.

"Thought I had you behind me still," he said. "I was talking to air." He handed her a red halter and lead and said, "You can bring in Ginger."

Ginger was the sorrel mare Cielle loved to ride. She clipped the lead rope to the halter and swung it over her shoulder. Mr. Mitchell held open the metal gate and closed it behind her.

"I almost forgot," he said, and handed Cielle a carrot from his front pocket. He kicked a clod of dirt and it broke into a fine dust. "One of the driest years on record."

The pasture was bumpy and rocky and could twist an ankle easily. The air was warm and carried the smell of sweet grass up from the swale that dipped down to a still body of water and a stand of trees where Ginger stood. Her tail slapped at flies and her withers quivered. The ticking of grasshoppers and cicadas was all around. A sound that reminded Cielle of her mother starting the gas oven. The sound of fire.

Cielle walked down the hill and watched her step. Buttercups and clover bloomed bright and low to the ground. She bent and picked a buttercup and held it to her chin, but forgot the reason why you did that. Her father knew. She smelled honeysuckle as she neared the trees, and the air cooled, like a cold pocket of water in a lake.

"Here, Ginger," she said, and came up on the left side of the mare. "Here I am, girl."

Mosquitoes swarmed by the water and buzzed around her head. Cielle ran her hand down Ginger's neck, which felt soft and firm, and she thought of the blood charging beneath.

"I love you, Ginger," she said, and petted her hard. "You're so good."

She put her cheek to Ginger's neck and felt tightness rising in her chest, tightness moving up into her throat, and then her throat gone itchy and salty, her cheek muscles pulling back, and her eyes filling up, her eyes wet.

"I love you so much," she said, and held the carrot out in the palm of her hand.

Ginger raised her head and took the carrot, and Cielle's arms shook as she adjusted the halter. Cielle led her up the hill toward the gate, toward Mr. Mitchell and the barn, where she would walk Ginger into her stall, slip off her halter, and let her lie down in darkness.

CHAPTER TWO

Cielle's mother came to the Mitchells' door, her curly brown hair wiry and unkempt, her eyes puffy and red, and she took Mr. Mitchell outside. An hour had passed between Cielle being home and at the Mitchells'. Cielle sat quietly on the couch and ran her fingers over the white-painted windowsill. The hum and turn of the heavy fan and the shake-beat of the crickets filled the quiet. She waited for her mother to come inside and announce the news, for everyone to break, but instead the truck peeled over the gravel and dirt and pulled away.

Her mother and Mr. Mitchell didn't return for an hour, and when they did her mother's face was pale and sweaty like a wet piece of potter's clay. It was near dark; there was a twilight purple sky and stars were visible — points of light that were small and clear and steady. They were all called to sit in the living room, and her

22

mother stood, straightened her shoulders, and exhaled loudly. "There's been an accident," she said. Then she cried out, almost like a yell, and bit her fist as tears came.

Mr. Mitchell stood in the doorframe with crossed arms and dropped his chin to his chest and cleared his throat as if he were going to say something. Instead, he rubbed his eyes and sat down next to Cielle on the couch. He picked up her hand and put his other hand over hers, as if it were a butterfly he'd caught.

"What do you mean?" Helen asked.

"Your father and the tractor," her mother said. Her voice caught in her throat. "He's gone."

"The tractor?" Cielle looked at her mother, who nodded yes, as if she believed it.

Cielle felt Mr. Mitchell's body twitch and shake. His neck and cheeks were blotchy red from too much heat, from emotion. Blood vessels, blood flow, life. She focused on the weave of her new summer linen pants, then on the shiny brown of her lace-up ankle boots, and the pine floorboards under her feet. She watched him from the corner of her eye as he tried to hold sadness in his body so she wouldn't see. But she felt sadness, like a current running from his hand into hers, grief in his quick jerks. Mr. Mitchell's face was red and parts were wet with sweat. He smelled of onions and dirt. Cielle pulled at her bottom lip. She felt weighted and limbless. Mr. Mitchell put his own hand over his mouth, shook his head from side to side, and turned to face the wall.

"Bodie," Mr. Mitchell said, "get their overnight bag from the backseat of the truck."

Everyone cried. No one spoke.

Her mother remained standing. Helen sat outside with Bodie. Mr. Mitchell put his head in his hands. Mrs. Mitchell busied herself. She cried but made no noise. She collected dishes and silverware and linen napkins and set them in the middle of the table, took out chicken and mashed potato leftovers from the icebox, and beans in a bowl of cold water. She held the bowl and raised her eyebrows at Cielle, so Cielle went and snapped the ends of the beans and laid them on a towel on the counter. Out the window, the bell-shaped metal light that hung from the Mitchells' shed was on, and it cast a wide glow of yellow light on the driveway and on a nearby oak tree. Swarms of insects darted under the light, frantic and confused, as if they didn't know what was in front of them or where they should go.

Mrs. Mitchell gathered Cielle's pile of beans and put them into a pot. "Let's get these cooked and let's eat." She put her homemade butter and wheat bread on the table.

Mr. Mitchell took three glasses and a bottle of whiskey out of another cabinet. He poured the whiskey and handed a glass to Cielle's mother and one to Mrs. Mitchell.

They ate with little conversation. The sounds were of silverware on plates, chewing, bread ripping, and glasses clinking. Bing Crosby sang "Black Moonlight" over the radio. Mrs. Mitchell got up and put a raspberry pie on the table. Cielle accepted a large piece and ate every bite. She was ravenous, and as she filled herself, she felt her body and mind come back to her and she felt exhaustion. Her eyes were heavy. Her whole body was heavy.

"Whenever you're finished," Mrs. Mitchell said, "please be excused. I put you and the girls together in the guest room."

Cielle's mother smiled. "Thank you, Dorothy."

The music cut out and a sonorous newsman's voice came over the radio. "On this day, July 19, 1943, the Allies bombed Rome," he said.

"What a shame," Mrs. Mitchell said.

"They have to do what they have to do," Mr. Mitchell said.

"But to destroy so much history."

"It might be the only way to stop the madness," he said, and Cielle caught Mr. Mitchell's nod at Bodie, as if this were a matter only men could understand, as if destruction and death were the only ways to restore peace and set things right.

Bodie had talked about the Army Air Corps because he loved planes and wanted to fly them, and he wanted to help restore freedom and save lives, but Helen wouldn't have it. Boys were leaving and weren't coming back. Two boys from Boaz had already died in the war.

"That's foolish," her mother said.

"What's that?" Mr. Mitchell asked.

"War," she said. "Dying."

"Sometimes it's necessary," Bodie said.

"You're too young to know what's necessary," she said.

"I don't know," Bodie said.

"I don't think you do," her mother said.

"Maybe we need war for peace," Bodie said.

"There's no such thing as peace. Never has been." She shook her head back and forth quickly. "Never."

"Well —" Bodie began.

"That's enough," Mr. Mitchell said. "That's enough. It's late."

That night, Cielle shared a queen-sized bed with Helen and her mother. Helen was in the middle and they had nothing but a sheet over them. The night air was hot and utterly still and the heat wrapped around them. The window was open and the crickets were loud. Within minutes Cielle heard her mother snoring lightly.

Helen turned on her side toward Cielle, and she touched Cielle's cheek. "Did you see him?"

There was a half-moon casting dull shadows into the room, and the wrought-iron bed frame was a delicate curving black silhouette at the foot of the bed. Cielle felt a pressure on her chest she hadn't felt before, something running and bearing down inside her. She pressed her hand just under her breast, at her heart, feeling for irregularity. She pressed harder and felt better, as if that might keep her heart in place, beating slower, as it should.

"Go to sleep," her mother said.

"Did you see him?" Helen asked.

"Stop talking," her mother said. "Erase it from your mind and go to sleep."

"You can't say that," Cielle said.

"I just did." Her mother turned on her side and faced away from them.

Cielle wished her mother would wrap her arms around her, and hold her feet in the wells of her ankles or between her thighs, the way she did when she and Helen were small. Cielle knew she was too old, but she felt small and in need of being held, in need of being her mother's daughter and of being loved. She didn't make a noise or shake. Tears simply emptied from her eyes, and she let them wet her face and the pillow. She cried for her father being gone forever, and for not knowing who in the world would love them and take care of them the way he had.

CHAPTER THREE

Cielle stood at the back of the room at the funeral home while men and women in black suits walked up the aisle and paid their respects. The top of her father's head rose up just above the wood of the coffin — his nose, his dark hair in place, and his white and waxy forehead. She wondered if he looked more like himself and considered walking up so she could wipe out the image of him hanging from the rafters. But she stood her ground, her arms tightly crossed over her chest, a small white calla lily pinned to her black dress above her left breast.

The rest of her family sat in folding chairs in the front with their heads down. It was a Saturday, five days past, and throughout the morning people from town came to say they were sorry. There were people she had known her whole life and some people she'd never seen before, and there in the third row in the middle she saw Darren Olsen, whom she thought she could love. She'd had a crush on him for years. He sat next to a woman who must have been his mother. His mother was a counselor, who, she had heard, had studied psychology in Chicago and was now helping returning veterans. Cielle had never met her before. The Olsens kept to themselves, although Darren's grandfather, Old Mr. Olsen, was well known. He owned most of the land in the area — it was land he'd bought from people during the Depression and leased back to people to farm. Many families wondered if they'd ever be able to afford to buy their land back, land that had been in their family for generations.

Darren wore a dark gray suit; she'd never seen him dressed up before. He turned and looked at Cielle, as though he'd felt her eyes on him. He nodded. He was handsome and she was glad he was there. His mother turned and she gave Cielle a small smile, put her hand on Darren's head, and they turned back around. His mother was pretty despite the smudged mascara beneath her eyes. She pulled Darren closer and he leaned his head to hers. He had the same dark eyes as his mother.

Amish men and women sat still and upright, their hands in their laps, or stood silently among the crowd. Every year, her father had hired Amish men to help with the cutting and baling of hay, and every season a boy not much older than Helen helped with the cows, pigs, and harvesting of crops.

"Honey." Her grandmother put her hand on Cielle's elbow from behind. Her hand was cool and soft.

"I can't look," Cielle said. "I already know he's dead. I don't need to be reminded of it." The room was stuffy and perfume smells made Cielle light-headed and queasy. Her palms and neck were damp with sweat.

"Your father was good on the farm." Her grandmother coughed. "Always careful. This is such a shame." She wore her graying hair in a neat bun, and smelled powdery and brassy.

Her grandmother had been the daughter and wife of a farmer. She'd had six children, and now Cielle's father was the second to die.

A flute played and Mr. Skaar, the funeral director, opened the doors to the outside to mark the end of the viewing. The near-noon light came in like a flash and Cielle squinted. Her grandmother nodded at the front doors and the outside light and said, "I need some air." Cielle walked with her down the cement steps that were covered in green felt carpet.

"I can't believe he's dead," Cielle said.

Her grandmother turned away. The ground where they stood was full of dried tufts of grass. Cielle shifted her stance. People trickled out of the funeral home and her grandmother turned back, tears falling down her face.

"I haven't cried in three years," she said. "Not since your grandfather died." She wiped her face on her sleeve and mascara blotted her silk shirt like a pen leaking ink. "I hate crying."

"I'm sorry."

Cielle's mother and Helen came out of the funeral home and waved at them. Then a young Amish man left his circle of people and approached her mother. He took off his hat and looked at the ground. He looked familiar. Her mother patted his forearm, said something, and he nodded and put his hat back on. Then Cielle remembered where she'd seen him before — at the farmers' market in Richland Center.

At that farmers' market the June before in Richland Center, the June when life still had a solid shape, normalcy, and comfort to it, Cielle remembered her mother had pointed to him and said, "See that young man?" He'd waved to them and Cielle thought he waved because he was Amish, friendly, and used to people staring and pointing.

"That young man," her mother had said, and smiled, "you can tell he's unmarried because he's clean-shaven. He's a handsome young man, isn't he?" Her mother had taken her by the elbow, as her grandmother had, and pulled her toward his market stand. "Why don't we buy something from him? We've pointed and waved, for God sakes."

"Mother, don't embarrass me," Cielle had said.

"Don't be silly," she'd said.

When they were close to him, only feet away, Cielle noticed the gray stitches that sewed his shirt together, like stitches in a wound. Like knowing what held a person together and kept them from falling apart. Wide, gray stitches in his navy blue shirt and suspenders.

"Good morning," he said, and tipped his hat.

"This is my youngest, Cielle," her mother said, pushing Cielle forward by the small of her back.

"My pleasure." He shook her hand and Cielle blushed. "I'm John."

"Cherries?" her mother asked.

"Not yet, they're almost ready. You'll have to come back next week."

"Then I'll come back next week," she said.

"I'll set some aside for you, Mrs. Jacobson."

"That would be fine," she had said. "We'd like that very much."

Across the funeral home lawn, her mother and the young man parted ways, and then Helen and her mother drove away toward home. Her grandmother was busy looking in the other direction and wiping away her tears, so Cielle said she'd forgotten something inside and that she'd meet her at the car.

Everyone was gone from the building except her father lying in the open coffin at the front of the viewing room. She made the sign of the cross over her face and chest. His skin was pale, clean-shaven, and smoothed out with makeup. His chest was puffed up in his navy pin-striped suit. There was a faint line of bruising under the collar of his shirt from where the rope had pulled tight, held all his weight, and took the life right out of him. She touched his forehead, saw a gash on the left side of his temple she

34

hadn't noticed before. He was cold, and his skin didn't feel like skin. It was hard and rubbery, like chilled chicken skin.

His hands lay one crossed over the other, the way they put all dead people's hands — quietly respectful, resting. She put her hand on his. It seemed a wonder how many people lived as long as they did, how they ever survived as a brittle pile of bones covered with such fragile skin.

His pants leg was wrinkled, so she smoothed it down and his leg felt hard. She lifted the pants leg and it was wood from the knee down. It was filler. Half his leg was gone. Her breath caught. A man cleared his throat from the back of the room and it startled her. She pulled the pants leg back down to his sock. She turned to see Mr. Skaar.

"You're surprised?" he asked, and shook his head. "The accident took it from the knee down."

Cielle didn't say anything.

"Your mother forgot to leave money for the service and upcoming burial," he said.

"How much does she owe?"

"She'll know." Mr. Skaar took a step toward Cielle.

"Okay," Cielle said. "I'll let her know."

"Your mother's a busy woman and you're

35

a big girl, so you might want to bring it by for her. Save her the trouble."

"It'll get to you."

"You might also tell her Mr. Olsen was inquiring about the details."

"Old Mr. Olsen?"

"The land man, who lives down in Muscoda. Tell your mother he's asking questions and looking for facts."

She looked back at her father and wondered what bigger mess was coming.

"I'm sorry for your loss, Cielle," Mr. Skaar said. "It's not fair when people leave us."

Cielle's grandmother drove her wide black sedan to their farmhouse. She drove slowly, and wound up the hill on the skinny road. The road was shaded and darkened by the trees as if they were passing through a tunnel, and there were brief bright clearings that opened to houses and sweeping fields.

"Is your mother worried about the farm?" her grandmother asked.

"I imagine so."

"This has been a hard dry spell. It's been twenty years since I've seen it this bad."

Cielle tilted her head out toward the window. When the sun hit her face, her brown hair blew back and whipped around her chin, and there were traces of red in the light.

"Maybe there's nothing to worry about," her grandmother said.

"I doubt that," Cielle said.

"What doesn't kill you makes you stronger."

"Maybe." One thing she knew from the time she was a little girl was that she wanted to be seen and known. She wanted recognition. She wanted to be noticed. She wanted to be strong.

Cars and trucks crowded the driveway. Their house looked as it always did: crisp and clean with the black shutters against the white clapboard, and despite the drought, her mother kept red and pink potted geraniums on the front porch, and blue hydrangeas bloomed along the house and in the side yard. The lawn was cut short, and was yellowed and burned in spots from the drought and the sun, but nothing looked out of place.

The barn stood off to the side and she had a hard time looking at the structure. The rush in her chest returned, she felt a small sharp pain in her back, and she had to catch her breath. For the first time she was aware of the uncertainty of everything.

Her cousins threw a baseball in the front yard and aunts and uncles carried food and drinks, and set up the picnic table in the side yard under the tree. Her relatives hadn't been together in one place since her grandfather's death three years earlier. They all lived within two hours' driving but never planned reunions, and so here they were, brought together by grief and loss.

Cielle took two deviled eggs from a tray on the counter and walked to the front yard. Her older cousin Katherine had the croquet set next to her, her hands on her hips, waiting for their male cousins to quit throwing the baseball on the front lawn and move out of the way so she could set up the course.

Cielle stood just behind her, took a bite off the end of one egg, and said, "I'll help you set up."

Katherine jumped. "I didn't see you, you scared me."

"The back yard is good for catch," Cielle said to the boys. "It's flatter." The boys shuffled around to the back yard, mumbling.

"In a few years they'll play with us," Katherine said.

"I know," Cielle said.

Katherine was the oldest of the cousins, and was easy and kind. She was a sophomore at the University of Wisconsin in Madison, and studied literature. She spread the equipment out on the grass — metal hoops, colored wooden balls and mallets.

"We're short a mallet or two," she said. "Yellow and red."

They were in the barn. Cielle could picture the corner where she and Helen had put them after their last game.

"All right," Cielle said, and ate the other deviled egg. "I know where they are."

Cielle walked straight toward the barn as if her legs weren't beneath her, as if she floated there. *It's just the barn, it's just the barn,* she chanted to herself. When she was at the door her chest was tight again and impossibly heavy. She stood, stuck. *Open the door. Walk through the door. Get the mallets. Walk out.* Cielle looked toward the house. Her mother stood there very still, with a drink in her hand, watching her.

Cielle unlatched the hook, slid the barn door open, and shut it behind her. She held her breath, kept her eyes down, and moved toward the mallets, but then stopped and looked up and around the whole place: soft dirt, bales of hay, flies buzzing through the musty hot air, and a swallow chirping above. It was just a barn, nothing more. She knew she shouldn't be afraid of it. She took a deep breath and sat on the hay bale closest to her, in the quiet, the voices outside muted.

Before her best friend Jillian moved to St. Louis in April, Jillian had said, "My mother keeps telling me to remember what's important, that this isn't the end of the world."

"What's that supposed to mean?" Cielle had asked.

"That life goes on," she had said, and shrugged. They sat on Cielle's bed and looked at each other.

"I guess," Cielle had said. "I guess it's not the end of the world."

Jillian had run her hand over Cielle's bedspread, and tears had fallen from her eyes. "That's what she says."

Cielle missed Jillian and wished she were in Boaz. Cielle was friendly with her classmates, but Jillian had been her one good friend. Cielle had always been shy and a loner, and she hadn't expected her sadness when Jillian left. She didn't know why adults made leaving people and moving on sound easy, like the natural order of things. What did others do when their loved ones left, especially when they weren't ready for them to leave?

There was a knock on the barn door and it slid open. Cielle's mother stuck her head in. "Why are you in there?" she asked. She kept her body outside of the barn walls.

"I'm looking for the croquet mallets," Cielle said.

"You don't look like you're looking for anything."

"I took a minute to sit down by myself in the quiet."

Her mother looked the barn up and down, her nose wrinkled.

"Do you want to come in?" Cielle asked.

"It's hot and smells in there, no, I don't want to come in."

"It's just a barn," Cielle said.

"Of course it's just a barn," her mother said. "Hurry up and get out of there before you pass out from the heat. Your grand-mother wants you to come play something on your violin." She left the door open and walked back to the house.

The red and yellow mallets leaned against the wall, just behind the bale where Cielle sat. She picked them up, held one in each hand, and walked to where her father had hung on Monday. The rope was gone, the tractor was gone, the wheelbarrow was in a new corner, and the dirt had been raked over. She walked to the spot where she had knelt below her father. She scuffed her shoe over the dirt. The soft layer brushed aside, and beneath it was dark. She stuck the head of the yellow mallet into it, ground it around, and lifted it for a look. She blew away a layer of dirt and there was a red smear on the wood.

"Shit." She banged the mallet on the ground, and it made a hollow thud. Her arms vibrated from the impact. She stood for moments, not moving. She felt sick, and set the yellow mallet behind the bale and covered it with hay.

Why? she thought. *Why bother? Why make it worse?*

No one talked about suicide. Even if people thought someone had killed himself or herself, they didn't ask. Mr. Daly had died the year before from a "hunting accident," even though everyone knew he was a hopeless drunk whose shotgun went off in his house. Tommy Bauer died by accidental drowning, even though everyone knew the war had made him crazy and that he had walked straight into the Mississippi with rocks in his pockets.

The hot air closed in, she felt lightheaded, and had to get out of the barn.

She told Katherine she was sorry but the mallets were missing, and then went inside and tuned her violin. She hadn't played for days. Her grandmother sat in the armchair in the living room by the window and sipped on iced tea with lemon and mint. Cielle sat on the couch across from her and slid rosin over her bow.

"I never could play anything," her grandmother said, crossing her legs and resting the drink on her knee. "I couldn't read music."

Every time her grandmother came to visit, she asked Cielle to play and they had this very same conversation. Cielle had been playing violin for five years now, and she was good. Since her school was small and there were only fifteen summer school students, Cielle had the music room to herself in the afternoons. She practiced after the geometry and physics classes she had to make up. Both classes were still hard for her the second time around, and she struggled to understand them. Matter, the interaction of forces and energy, and theories were not her strength. She understood literature and music. Things you could touch and see and hear.

"It's memorization and practice," Cielle said, and picked up the violin. She plucked each of the four strings to find its pitch and adjusted the tuning pegs.

"How do you even know what the right sound is when you're doing that?" her grandmother asked.

"She has bat-ears," Cielle's mother said from the kitchen. "She could tune and play in the dark."

"No, I couldn't," Cielle said. She lifted the violin, nestled her chin in the chin rest, and raised her bow. Her pinkie stuck out. Her mother sat on the arm of the chair next to her grandmother. Cielle looked at her mother and thought, *Who are you? What have you done?* Cielle slowly slid her bow over the strings.

"My favorite," her grandmother said.

Cielle played Pachelbel's Canon in D. Her grandmother closed her eyes and waved her hand back and forth in front of her with the music. Helen and Bodie came in through the back door. Soon aunts and uncles and even the younger cousins came inside to listen. Her grandmother smiled and looked peaceful, so Cielle kept playing. She played by memory, her fingers moving of their own accord. There was not a noise in the room except for the violin.

All the windows in the house were open and a cool gust of wind came in behind her mother and the top of her dress puffed full of air. Cielle played to the wind, to the darkening sky coming toward them, to her family gathered in one room, all her family, all part of her, together. *This is the sound of sadness,* she thought. *This is the sound of how the living remember the dead.* She played and played until a stronger gust of wind blew in and knocked over and broke a delicate clay vase on the side table, and then she stopped.

"The sky's real dark." One of her cousins pointed west with a baseball mitt still on his hand.

"Finally, some rain," Mr. Mitchell said.

"Wouldn't that be something," an uncle said.

Her grandmother stood. "Thank you for playing, Cielle." She clapped and looked around the room until everyone clapped. Cielle took a small bow.

"Let's bring lunch inside," Mrs. Mitchell said.

The adults went outside to bring in the food. Cielle stayed where she was and put her violin back in its case. The sky was still blue and bright over their farm, but the air was changing, cooling and blowing over the baked and wilting fields.

Cielle's mother balanced a loaf of bread and a wooden salad bowl. "Come here," she said. "Take this bread."

Cielle took the bread and her mother set the bowl on the kitchen table.

"That was lovely playing. You have good instincts." Her mother picked up the salad mixers and tossed the lettuce quickly and with force. A piece of lettuce flew out of the bowl onto the table. People streamed into the house with food, plates, glasses, silverware, tablecloths, and the room filled with chatter. Her mother picked up the piece of lettuce from the table and ate it.

Cielle had wanted answers since she was a small child. She wanted to know how the world was made, and why people said and did the things they did. She wanted to know her place in the universe, her purpose, and what it all meant. She wanted to know *why,* but no one ever had any answers for her. Her father had told her she should find her own answers and not rely on others' explanations of the world, and not to rely on others to tell her what to do or what was true. Her father had always made sense to her, until now.

"Mom, Mr. Skaar said you forgot to pay. He said you'd know how much it cost," Cielle said.

Her mother said nothing.

"He asked that I bring him the money."

"Why did he ask you?"

"To help you out."

"Fine. That's fine."

46

"He said to tell you Mr. Olsen from Muscoda is asking questions."

"Mr. Olsen from Muscoda?"

"I think Mr. Skaar knows the truth and Mr. Olsen wants it."

"He wants the truth?"

Cielle's grandmother walked in carrying a glass pitcher of lemonade in the crook of her arm, her other hand supporting the bottom. "I heard the word *truth*," she said.

"Of course you did," Cielle's mother said.

Her grandmother bent over and slowly set the pitcher on the table. "Take it from an old woman." Her grandmother wiped her hand on her skirt. "People have to live with their own lies."

Cielle had lied about small things before: about coming home late, not finishing homework, drinking beer. Nothing like what she knew her mother and grandmother were talking about. Nothing like what she was carrying around now: the kind of lies that created a deeper and darker crevice between people, the kind of lies that could never be taken back, the kind of lies that ruined lives. She thought lying wasn't about privacy but about choosing to be unknown, choosing to be anonymous, and sometimes about protection. She'd always thought the truth was worth knowing, but maybe she'd been wrong. Yet, she'd still rather know the truth than not. She'd rather know what part of her father and mother were a part of her.

"The only thing you want to know is when someone stops loving you," her grandmother said. "But you usually know long before they ever say a thing."

"You're right on that." Her mother cut the loaf of homemade bread with a long serrated knife.

"I know," her grandmother said.

Her mother placed the sliced bread into a basket, and then wiped her eyes dry with the dish towel. "I've got to roll up the windows before it rains." She made her way to the truck, her legs thin and pretty as she walked steadily over the grass and dirt in heels.

"Nothing romantic about love, Cielle," her grandmother said. "It's hard work to love somebody. Nobody ever tells you that. And it's hardest when they leave you without reason or warning."

A wind came and brown locust pods twirled down like propellers. Her mother opened the truck door, sat in the seat, shut the door, and rolled up the windows. She stayed in the truck, her hands on the wheel, as if she might drive straight out into the field and the woods beyond. Drive, drive fast, drive away.

"Let's start eating this food," her grand-mother said loudly. People milled toward the table. Mrs. Mitchell came in from outside, windblown.

"Should we wait for Mom?" Helen asked her.

"She needs a minute of quiet," Mrs. Mitchell said. "Let her be."

They ate. An hour later, when they were finished, her mother was still in the truck. Nearing three in the afternoon, the relatives packed up, some to make their train in Richland Center and others to drive home. They walked by the truck window and knocked and waved, but her mother didn't move. They worried and thought to stay, but her grandmother told them to go on home, and that she'd look after her. And so they left. The Mitchells stayed to help clean up. Her grandmother was staying for the burial the next day and however long she felt like staying beyond that.

The sky darkened and rain came in slow, big drops. Then the sky opened up and the rain fell hard and loud, as if hundreds of people were clapping in applause.

CHAPTER FOUR

Far off the sky turned a dark shade of green, like a bruise. The temperature dropped. Rain turned into hail the size of gumballs and tree branches swayed, snapped, and fell.

"Cellar," Mr. Mitchell yelled, "everyone go down into the cellar." He pointed to the cellar door, but Cielle looked outside for her mother, who was still in the truck.

"I'll get the windows shut," Helen said.

Cielle grabbed an umbrella and ran outside. She pulled on the driver's-side door but it was locked. The truck windows were fogged but she could make out her mother's form. Her arms were up high on the steering wheel and her head leaned against them as though she were napping.

"Mom." She pounded on the window. "Open up. We have to get to the cellar."

The window rolled down halfway. "It's okay, Cielle. Nothing ever hits our property."

"Get out of the truck."

A gust whipped and turned her umbrella inside out. The hail, now the size of small pebbles, hit and stung her arms and neck, pricking her skin. Cielle hunched over to shield her face, and righted the umbrella. A hailstone hit her cheek and her skin burned and her eyes watered. When she stood, her mother had rolled up her window and the door was still locked.

"Cielle," Mr. Mitchell yelled from the doorway. "Get in here. Anything could fall from that locust."

"My mother," Cielle yelled, and wasn't sure he could hear her. The noise from the hail and the wind was like yelling over a motor. "She won't unlock the door." She yanked on the handle again.

Mr. Mitchell pulled his coat up over his head and ran to her.

"This is no joke," he said. "Get inside now."

"Not without Mother."

Mr. Mitchell knocked on the window. It rolled halfway down again.

"Go away, Jim, and get Cielle inside."

"Olive, this isn't a false alarm. You can't stay in this truck. This isn't the time to be a pain in the ass." Mr. Mitchell reached his arm through the window and pulled up the lock. Her mother rolled up the window on him, but he was stronger and pushed down on the glass and opened the door.

"Jesus Christ," her mother said. "Leave me alone."

Thunder cracked and boomed. Cielle felt it in her chest like a drum.

Mr. Mitchell pulled her out of the truck. "Let's go," he said.

The hail slowed to sporadic drops, but Cielle held the umbrella over her mother anyway. Hail littered the drive and lawn like small white pebbles, and they crunched under their feet.

"Stop treating me like an invalid," she said. Cielle could tell she'd been crying; her eyelids were tender and swollen. She twisted in Mr. Mitchell's grip and wiped her nose on the back of her hand. Her hair was wild.

The hail stopped, and so did the wind.

"Hurry," Mr. Mitchell said.

It was damp, humid, and quiet in the cellar. There weren't any windows and it was dark, save the one candle glowing in the middle of the floor and around which everyone sat.

"Oh, thank God," Cielle's grandmother said as they came down the stairs. "You could have blown to Michigan in that truck."

Cielle sat next to Helen and Bodie, by the jars of raspberry and apricot jam, pickled vegetables and honey.

"Don't be dramatic," Cielle's mother said, and stood in front of everyone like a preacher. "Nothing ever hits our property." Her mother shook out her hair and smoothed it back, twisted it up, and tied it into a loose bun at the nape of her neck.

"Never say never," her grandmother said.

Her mother tapped her right heel on the cement floor. *Click click click.* Cielle wondered if she'd been drinking in the truck. Her shoe tapped faster. *Click click, click click, click click.* She breathed loudly in and out of her nose and reached into her dress pocket and pulled out a piece of writing paper folded into a square. She rotated the paper in a circle and touched each of the pointed edges with the tips of her forefingers. She looked at Cielle, pursed her lips, and then looked away. She smiled, held the paper up in front of her, shook her head no from side to side, and carefully unfolded it.

"What is that?" Cielle's grandmother asked.

"Olive, sit down," Mr. Mitchell said.

She folded the note back up and laid it on a stairstep. "I don't know what to say." She walked to the shelves, took a jar of dill pickles, and twisted off the top. She pulled a pickle out of the jar and the juice dripped onto the floor. Everyone looked at the note, but no one moved.

"I don't understand." Cielle's mother bit off half the pickle and chewed. Then she pointed the other half of the pickle at Mr. Mitchell. "How did this happen?"

"Don't say another word," Mr. Mitchell said. "Sit down."

"He wasn't supposed to die." Her mother threw the glass jar at the wall and it shattered.

Cielle's grandmother stood and lowered her mother down to sit, and held her, rocking her back and forth. "He wasn't supposed to die," she cried.

Helen reached out to Cielle's hand and held it. Cielle looked at her. Cielle didn't know how they would come out of this. She didn't know how her mother would be able to live with what she had done.

Suddenly air rushed above them like a waterfall and there was a deep pounding like the sound of a train coming full speed, something heavy and mean coming their way.

"Get close and lock arms," Mr. Mitchell said. "Put your head to your knees."

Cielle locked arms with Helen and Bodie,

closed her eyes, and pressed her head into her knees. *Not today, don't let this happen today.* She smelled jasmine perfume on Helen, the mildew and concrete of the cellar, the laundry soap on her dress, and the brine and vinegar of pickles.

Window glass popped and shattered above. There was a crack of thunder, and the house groaned in the wind. She imagined shingles flying off one after another, a deck of cards flung in the air. Then there was a crash and boom of something fallen, and Cielle felt it in her body.

"Something's down," her grandmother said.

"The locust," Bodie said.

"Something bigger," Mr. Mitchell said.

The roar above passed like a living thing in motion. Then there was silence. Her ears rang.

"Everyone stay put," Mr. Mitchell said. He scooped up the note, tucked it into his pocket, and went upstairs. Cielle followed. She shut the cellar door behind her and Mr. Mitchell turned and held her shoulders firmly; his hands were cool from resting on the concrete.

"Go back downstairs," he said.

"Give it to me." Cielle held out her hand, palm up.

There was a spot near his upper lip where he'd missed shaving, and the stubble was a perfect small dark edge. It reminded her of a patch of grass missed by the mower. He had a red broken blood vessel under his eyelid, small and bright. A little jagged river of blood.

"I want to know what he wrote. Give it to me."

He opened his mouth to speak, his mouth dark and empty like a cave, but no sound came out. He reached into his pocket and held out the note. She took it and looked past him out the window, and her insides dropped and hollowed.

"No," she said. "No, no, no."

Mr. Mitchell turned. "Jesus Christ," he said.

The barn was gone. There was a heap of splintered wood, as if a string had been pulled and the barn collapsed in place. Gone. A pile of red boards, of pine beams, of hay, of a tractor, a rope, a wheelbarrow, a bloodied yellow croquet mallet somewhere buried underneath. The world needed to wipe out this place where something bad had happened. The barn couldn't be there anymore.

A large locust limb lay across her grand-mother's car. It sat on the hood in a deep dent and the front tires were flattened. She took the note, kicked open the screen door, and went outside. The heat had returned to the air and a swallow sat on the roof of the crushed car. The tires hissed leaking air. She sat on the hood of the car and the swallow flew away toward a triangle of bright blue sky — it was electric-blue, glass-bottle-blue, a jewel behind the dark clouds.

The house was unscathed by the tornado except for two broken windows. Cielle was comforted by the sight of her bedroom and her things. In the corners of the mirror over her dresser she'd stuck photos of her friends, her grandparents, and one of her, Helen, and her parents in front of the Christmas tree last winter. The tree's lights had a soft fuzzy glow. On top of her dresser sat a silver box with her initials engraved in cursive on the top — LPJ — for Lucille Patricia Jacobson. Inside she kept jewelry and keepsakes. A note from Darren Olsen that read, *You play the violin well, you have pretty green eyes.* A dried four-leaf clover. A smooth and shiny piece of green glass she'd found by the creek. A gold locket from her dead maternal grandmother, Viola; a woven bracelet from Helen; her mother's lace handkerchief; and the delicate wooden bird pin her father had made for her. Next to her box sat a fluted quartzite spearpoint from the banks of Mill Creek.

She and her father had often walked to Mill Creek looking for remains left behind and not yet discovered from the Boaz mastodon. "A wash-out rainfall uncovered the beast," her father had said. "Farmer found it in 1897, part of the skeleton poking out from the mud." And so they went down through a meadow to the creek on dry days and wet to look for bones: monster bones, bones as big as tree trunks, tusks like carved wooden horns. She imagined the elephantlike animal with shaggy hair roaming Boaz, and wondered if anything looked the same twelve thousand years before, if there had been humans and if they spoke a language close to hers, and how the mastodon became extinct. What made it disappear forever? Could anyone ever know for sure? History said maybe it was hunters or maybe it was the ice age ending, and the earth warming and becoming uninhabitable, a shift beyond their control. And maybe that was her father: an animal that couldn't live in his body anymore.

Her father was fascinated with all things old, lost, buried — and because of that, so was she. She loved the idea of discovery, reclamation, and a continuum. That April she and her father had crouched along the riverbank feeling for treasure. Their hands were wet and covered in mud and clay. Skunk cabbage bloomed new and shiny green, and small yellow flowers blanketed the ground like thousands of tiny yellow buttons. Cielle moved her hand back and forth over the ground, moving layer after layer of earth. When a rock came up, she inspected it and put it aside in a small pile like prayer stones. Then she felt a sharp point. At first she thought it was a piece of broken glass, but it was a gray spearpoint carved out of quartzite and as big as her forearm.

"Look at that," her father said. "Unbelievable."

"What is it?"

"A weapon," he said. "Maybe what killed the mastodon. You've made your first discovery."

Cielle ran her hands over its serrated edges. It was heavy and she held it in the crook of her arm like a baby.

Her father scooted over to her to look and stood behind her with his hands on her shoulders. "You're a natural."

She looked up at him. "If we didn't come down here all the time, this might have stayed buried. No one would know it was here."

"The only way to find something is to look for something." He patted her shoulders. "Hell of a find."

The dead were always among the living. Just because she couldn't see them didn't mean they weren't there. She knew they were around her still; her father was around them still. The living pieced together meaning from what the dead left behind. That's how it always had been and always would be.

Mr. Mitchell told them to stay inside while he assessed the damage outside. Cielle busied herself. She folded her quilt and set it on the oak rocking chair in the corner of the room. She stripped her bed and put the sheets in the hallway. She did the same in Helen's room and peeked in Helen's closet to look at her dresses and blouses. She touched the peach silk dress Helen wore for her graduation in June, a gift from their well-off aunt Josie, her father's sister, who had also gifted them money for college. The silk was cool to the touch, and moved in her hand like water. It was the prettiest dress. Cielle wanted to try it on, but didn't want to rip or snag it by accident.

Then she went into her parents' room. She walked to her father's side of the bed, on the left near the closet. She lay facedown and smelled him on the pillow. It smelled like soap and the spice of his aftershave. She wanted to smell him forever. She sat up so her tears wouldn't wet the pillow.

"If you can hear me," she said, "I miss you."

Cielle knew her mother couldn't bear the smell of her missing father, so she folded their comforter and set it aside. She took the sheets off their bed, slowly, as if she might find her father underneath them. She left the pillowcase on her father's pillow and put it in her room on her bed, even though she knew washing the pillowcase wouldn't make her father disappear.

Cielle and Helen pinned the wet sheets on the clothesline to dry; the sheets smelled fresh and clean, and swayed gently. There was just enough light left in the day for them to dry before dark. The sisters walked into the house through the back door, and Helen held up her arm for Cielle to stop, and turned and put her finger over her lips to keep quiet. They stood in the long narrow hall that led to the kitchen and listened to their mother and Mr. Mitchell.

"The way the numbers shake out, Olive, you could keep the farm for a year with a hired hand or two doing the work," Mr. Mitchell said.

"And then?" she asked.

"We can help you find work," he said. "Maybe find an apartment in town in Richland Center? Or maybe family could take you in?"

Cielle wondered about how the farm would run, but hadn't thought about leaving it. Richland Center was only eight miles away, a bigger town with some shops and restaurants, but it wasn't home.

"Is there enough so that Helen can still start college in Madison in the fall?" her mother asked.

"There's enough," Mr. Mitchell said, "from Lee's sister's education trust for the girls. But there may not be enough to stay on the farm for long while paying hired help."

Her mother leaned her head back and closed her eyes. "I heard Old Mr. Olsen's been asking questions."

"If Olsen gets wind it was anything other than an accident, he could cancel the buyback agreement. What Lee did is a crime, and could mean forfeiture of your estate."

"We should never have agreed to sell in the first place. Jacobson land for eighty years, and now soon to be gone. Nothing for my daughters. Nothing for my grandchildren. Shameful."

Cielle's father had talked history on their walks, and this was what she knew: Her great-grandfather, Andrew Hans Jacobson, came from Norway and settled their farm in 1863. He bought and tended the land, and passed it on to his son Gustave, who passed it on to her father, Lee. The year the American stock market crashed her father sold their land to Old Man Olsen, who'd had money, and bought up most of Richland County from people in need, and rented their land back to them. They could stay on their land, work their land, profit from their land, but it wasn't their land. Not rightfully. They paid monthly rent to Old Mr. Olsen. Even though the country had failed them, her father felt he'd failed. Land agreements were signed. Her father had spoken of it matter-of-factly. *We did what we had to do. You make a decision and try to live without regret. Maybe one day we can buy it back,* he'd said. *Then I can pass on to you what was yours.* She was old enough to know regret, and recognize in others the wish for something to be other

63

than what it was.

There was a knock at the front door. It was Mrs. Mack from down the hill dropping off food. Mrs. Mack cried and shook her head. "I'm glad you're safe. We saw the funnel and knew it was close to you. First Lee, now your barn. I'm so sorry," she said, weeping. "I'd made this for you yesterday."

Helen walked into the kitchen and Cielle followed her.

Her mother came back in and set the glass dish on the counter. "You'd think it was her husband who died," she said. "Good God." Her mother wiped a strand of hair off her forehead.

"Laundry is done," Helen said.

Mr. Mitchell stood and smoothed down his pants and cleared his throat. "Everyone knew Lee, Olive. He meant a lot to a lot of people."

"Still, she doesn't need to blubber on my doorstep."

"He was a good man. He'll be missed."

"He is missed," she said.

"Cielle and Helen should know what's happening," Mr. Mitchell said.

"Fair enough." Her mother bunched up her lips and wiped her neck with a handkerchief. Then she picked up the glass dish and held it up in front of her. "It's lasagna," she said. "Mrs. Mack is a good cook." She opened the icebox and put it inside.

"Where's your grandmother?" her mother asked.

"Tending the garden," Cielle said.

Mr. Mitchell stood. "I need to get home. A lot of debris to clean up on the farm. Call if you need us." He walked to his truck and Cielle felt nervous with him leaving. This was the first time she was alone with her mother and Helen since her father's death. The house was shadowed and quiet inside.

"Girls, come sit down in the living room." Her mother sat in the middle of the couch and patted the cushions for them to sit on either side.

"Tomorrow is the burial service at the Five Points Cemetery." Her mother's jaw was firm and she did not look at either of them.

Cielle watched the dust particles float in the stream of light that shone through the window. Her house, her skin, the light in the sky, and the leaves on the trees all seemed more alive than ever, and she was more aware of herself and everything, in vibration, breathing, part of something bigger.

"I need you to help with the farm. We need to see what survived. I need you to check on and help care for the animals in the coming weeks," her mother said.

The animals needed food. Pens needed cleaning. Chicken eggs needed to be collected. Alice and Minnie, their Holsteins, hadn't been milked in days. Bart and Tulip and their six piglets were probably starving.

Her mother waved her hand for them to go. "We need to keep up around here. We have to take care of this farm. I know it's been a long day, but we need to see what's left. I can't keep it up all on my own."

Cielle and Helen changed their clothes. They pulled on their rubber boots just outside the front door. The heat was oppressive again — thick, damp, and exhausting.

"Guess we're full-time farmers now," Helen said.

"We always have been," Cielle said.

The chicken coop and pigpens were behind the fallen barn, down toward the edge of the field. They walked into the coop first. If the eggs weren't collected, the hens would brood and the eggs would hatch.

"Do you want the gloves?" Cielle asked. "You're better at holding Matilda while I take her eggs."

Helen put on the thick canvas gloves that

went up to the middle of her forearm. She grabbed for Matilda, but Matilda bounced around and her feathers prickled up.

"Oh, nuts," Helen said. "Come on, bird. We can't have any babies this week."

Helen lunged forward and missed her again. Matilda was too quick. She screamed and clucked, and the rest of the hens screamed and clucked. Cielle laughed.

"It's not funny," Helen said.

"Yes, it is," Cielle said.

"Well, get over here. Get closer. You can grab the eggs while I keep her on the other side of the coop."

Cielle moved closer to the nest. There were two eggs. Helen blocked Matilda and Cielle took the eggs quickly and put them into an egg crate.

"Once I go to college, I'll never farm again," Helen said. "I won't miss this."

Cielle moved over to the next nest. "Lift old Harriet up for me," she said. "She's sitting right on top of who knows how many eggs."

Helen reached for Harriet, and the hen was easy. She didn't wiggle or hiss and it was as though she were sleeping.

"I'm never going to live on a farm or in the country again," Helen said.

"Good for you." Cielle gathered three eggs

and set them in the crate.

The coop didn't need to be cleaned out. The straw was fresh and there were few droppings. Her father must have cleaned everything, fixed everything, made sure all was in place beforehand. They finished collecting the eggs and then Cielle filled buckets full of feed. Helen filled bins with fresh water for the birds. At the edge of the coop Cielle leaned down and emptied the bucket of feed for the chickens to come eat.

Though she had done this chore since she was ten, it was her least favorite. For the longest time she had wanted to cut and bale the hay, but her father said she wasn't tall enough or strong enough to man the tractor.

"Shit," Helen said from the other side of the coop. "Three dead chickens."

"Dead?"

"Dead." She held one up by its foot. "Probably overheated and not enough water." Helen's shirt was wet and smeared with dirt. "I'm going to live in a house or an apartment with small, tidy yard. No animals, no crops, no cow, chicken, or pig shit. Just a neat little house near town or the city."

"Stop telling me how much you hate this place," Cielle said. "We'll have to leave it soon enough."

"Mom would never leave this place," Helen said.

"You ready for the pigs?"

"She won't leave the farm." Helen pulled her hair back tightly and tied it into a knot on the top of her head.

"Weren't you listening? She won't have a choice," Cielle said. "Without Dad to run things and with us needing more hired hands, it can't last."

"It's not Dad's fault," Helen said. "Don't blame everything on Dad."

Cielle stopped and Helen kept walking. *But it is his fault,* she wanted to say. Helen's boots were too big for her thin calves and she looked like she might take a step and come right out of them. Helen kept walking toward the pigpen and dismissively waved her hand in the air without turning around. Helen had always been good at pretending and not looking at what was. Cielle carried the chickens out of the coop and set them aside to bury later in the woods.

The still air was close and wet and heavy. The grass was stiff as it dried and died. It seemed a miracle that rain could bring it back to life and it seemed impossible there had been so little rain. So much was dying.

Cielle followed Helen over the bumpy

ground. The bucket swung back and forth and hit her hip with each step. Her brow beaded with sweat, her neck was damp, and her legs cooked in the rubber boots.

The vegetable garden would be a struggle to keep alive. The plants wilted in the early evening sun, and she felt that tiredness in her own limbs. She tingled with heat. Her parents had started the garden before she was born, and taught her how to tend it, and Cielle vowed to water it every morning and night. She wouldn't let it die. There were tomatoes, potatoes, beans, summer squashes, lettuces, peas, carrots, radishes, broccoli, cauliflower, basil, mint, chives, rosemary, and sage. There was food to feed them. Sustenance. Growth. Life.

Cielle caught up with Helen at the pigpen. "Don't do that."

"Do what?" Helen scrunched up her face and pinched her nose. "Pig stink is the worst stink."

"Don't make me the villain," Cielle said.

"You always twist things around, Cielle."

"How am I twisting things around?"

"You always do."

"What are you talking about? Did you just overhear the same conversation?" Cielle filled a bucket with more feed. Their largest and oldest pig, Vernon, nudged her calf for food. "Hold on, Vernon." She pushed back with her leg. He was almost as large as her but three times as heavy.

"It was an accident. No one's to blame. Don't make this harder for the rest of us," Helen said.

"Are you just hearing only what you want to hear?"

"I'm not hearing anything."

"Maybe that's the problem."

"What's your problem? You say things that upset people. Why are you trying to cause trouble?"

Vernon nudged Cielle again, his round pink snout twitched, and his brown human-like eyes looked up at her. She poured the feed into the trough and Vernon trotted over and stood on her left boot. A sharp shock of pain hit her toes and shot up her leg. She felt warmth and a numbing tingle. Cielle hit him on the back with the bucket but he was too busy eating. "Off!" she yelled. "Move!"

"Easy," Helen said.

Cielle kicked Vernon with her other foot. Kicked him three times in his side as hard as she could. "Move," she yelled.

Helen pulled on Vernon's leg to get him to lift it.

When Vernon lifted off her, she hopped backward on one leg and kept her foot dangling above the ground. She threw the bucket at Vernon.

"He's just a hungry pig," Helen said.

"Pigs aren't stupid." Tears ran down Cielle's cheeks. "And now I can't walk."

"You can walk," Helen said. "You're fine."

"Four hundred pounds just stood on my toes for an hour."

"For two seconds."

Cielle leaned against a wood beam. Tears kept coming. She didn't know she had that much water in her head. Her nose snotted and ran, and she wiped her nose on the back of her hand and her hand on her pants. She inched back and sat on a bale of hay.

Helen moved around Vernon and knelt in front of Cielle. She grabbed her bootheel and gently pulled the boot off her foot. She rolled Cielle's sock down her ankle, down from her heel, and slid it off. Cielle looked at her foot. Helen handed her the sock and Cielle wiped her nose with it. Her toes were red. The bruise would deepen and turn black and blue in no time.

"It's going to hurt," Helen said, "but I don't think anything broke. Feet are resilient."

"I hurt all over."

"Let's go ice it."

Cielle held on to Helen's arm and pulled

herself up. Helen put her arm around Cielle's waist and Cielle hopped back to the house on her good foot. She sat on the couch with her leg up. Her foot was tender and throbbing. Helen put a towel full of ice chips on the top of it and Cielle flinched.

"Ignoring and avoiding might work for you, but it doesn't work for me," Cielle said. "If you'd rather pretend things are a certain way, rather than how they really are, then fine."

"That is fine," Helen said. "You think things are messier than they are. You're digging for something that doesn't exist. You're wasting your time."

Cielle wanted to tell her that their father had killed himself and their mother was a liar, but she couldn't say it. It wouldn't come out.

For dinner they ate the lasagna that Mrs. Mack had brought by that afternoon. Then their mother rose, having only eaten half of what was on her plate.

"I'm going to take a bath and go to sleep so I can put on a good face tomorrow," she said. "Get some rest." She walked toward the stairs. The ceiling lamp hanging above the table felt like a spotlight to Cielle, too bright, all on her.

Her grandmother rose to clear the table.

"People are meeting at the lake tonight," Helen said. "Want to go? Get out of here?"

"I don't know," Cielle said. "I'm tired."

"I found some of dad's homemade beer," she said. "It's in the cellar."

"I hate the cellar."

"Well, I'll get it from the cellar."

Cielle looked up at the ceiling, at the light, and squinted. She loved her sister, but sometimes didn't know if she liked her. She wished they saw the world the same way. She wanted an ally and an unbreakable bond but she didn't have that with Helen, and there was nothing she could do to change it.

"What else would you do? Sit here alone while everyone sleeps?" Helen stood and put her hands on her hips. "Clean the dishes and get your jacket. I'll get the beer. We'll drive to the lake, see our friends, and try to think about something else."

"Go ahead, girls. Go be with your friends," her grandmother said.

Helen drove. There was still daylight at the edges of the trees through the woods. The sky was a light blue ring fading to dark, a color that always made Cielle think of a metal rim and about what was at the edge of the earth. It made her think about how big the world was, how much of it she'd never seen, and about all the other people living their lives at that exact same moment. She wondered how many other girls had just lost their father, and were looking at that very same piece of sky.

"You smell like jasmine," Cielle said.

"Trudy gave me a small bottle for graduation, she bought it in Chicago." Trudy was Helen's best friend. Her father was a surgeon at the hospital in Richland Center, and their family was wealthy. Aside from their house in Boaz, they had a house on Green Lake and an apartment in Chicago. Helen got to spend time with them in both of those places. Trudy was going to Wellesley in the fall.

"It's nice," Cielle said.

"Here." Helen held out her wrist. "Rub."

Cielle rubbed her wrist against Helen's. Now she smelled like jasmine too: fresh, clean, like springtime, like something exotic.

"What did you give Trudy?"

"I made her an abstract painting. It looks like red barns in cornfields. Some Wisconsin for her to take to Massachusetts."

Helen was a wonderful painter, but Cielle knew she'd always keep painting as a hobby and never as something serious to pursue. Helen was practical and had a plan. She wanted to marry someone successful and have a family. She wanted to live in Chicago and have a lake house. She wanted to wear cashmere sweaters in the winter and silk in the summer.

"Are you excited to go to college?" Cielle asked.

"I can't wait. I get to start all over. You can come visit," she said. "We can eat whatever we want, go to a fraternity party or to see a band, and swim in Lake Mendota."

"Maybe you'll still be there when I come for college."

"Maybe," Helen said. "But you're smarter than I am, and you have your violin."

Helen drove slowly, as she always did. Their windows were down and the soft night air blew their hair around as they passed fields and barns and homes with their warm yellow lights on inside. Signs of life.

"Who knows?" Cielle said. "Who knows what will happen?"

They turned down a dirt road through tall stands of pine and oak trees toward the lake. After two miles, there was an opening, and then the beach and a bonfire. There were close to fifteen people sitting and standing around the fire. As the girls pulled in, heads turned and some people waved.

Helen parked a good distance from them. Before she got out of the truck, she touched Cielle's arm. "Let's have a good time tonight," she said. "Like we're the girls we were before all this. Don't get serious and sad and make everyone uncomfortable."

Cielle opened her mouth to speak, then nodded okay. If that's what Helen wanted, she would try, but this was where she and Helen were different. Helen saw feelings as weakness, and Cielle did not. Cielle knew they couldn't be those girls they were before all this. Cielle knew she could fake her old self, smile and pretend she was at ease and that all was okay in the world, and so she would, to make Helen happy, and to make their friends feel comfortable. But why should she have to? She knew no one expected that, except Helen, who had always been a good faker.

Helen grabbed the beer from the flatbed. Cielle carried a wool blanket and limped behind Helen, only putting pressure on her left heel. Her toes felt like sad, smashed things in her shoe. As they got closer, fewer voices spoke and more people turned.

Trudy came out of the crowd, tears in her eyes, her arms held wide. She didn't say a word, but hugged Helen, and then waved

Cielle toward her and hugged them both. After Trudy, their friends all approached with hugs and condolences, and Helen and Cielle let them. When it was over, they all sat on the sand around the fire. The small moment of acknowledgment passed.

Helen opened her bottle of beer and held it up. "Here's to new beginnings," she said. Everyone raised a bottle. Cielle raised hers too, even though she wasn't sure what for. She didn't get a new beginning. She envied Helen's escape, where she could start over. She could already see Helen placing their father's death someplace else, someplace manageable, where she wouldn't have to look too closely or grieve too long. Cielle thought that if she were Helen she might do the same, and would be counting the days until leaving Boaz.

Darren Olsen came out of the shadows from the other side of the fire and sat next to Cielle. Blood rose in her face. He pulled his knees against his chest and held them with his arms. He had hair the color of polished chestnuts. "Cielle," he said, looking at the fire. "I'm sorry about your father. How are you?"

"Our pig stepped on my toes today."

"Anything break?"

"Helen doesn't think so, but they're

bruised and feel smashed."

"I've never broken a bone. My parents think it's a miracle."

"Maybe you're magic," Cielle said. "Or a superhero."

"That would be nice. Unbreakable Man."

"Miracle Magical Mending Man."

"If only." He picked up a stick and dragged it through the sand in circle and diamond shapes, and then picked at the rocks in the dirt and threw them at the fire. "Before we moved to Boaz, my older brother died," he said.

"I'm sorry."

"You miss them real bad, and then a little less, but it never leaves you. It becomes a new kind of hurt." His eyes were back on the fire. "Next week's the county fair, if you want to go Friday."

"Yeah," she said. "I like the fair. Friday's good."

"Okay," he said. "Good."

She felt comforted having him there; he felt like the promise of change.

"Thanks for coming to the viewing today," she said.

"Sure."

"Your mother's pretty. I hadn't ever seen her before today."

"My mother . . ." he said, but didn't finish his thought. He put his foot in the middle of the stick he held, broke it in half, and threw both pieces into the fire.

Trudy stood at the edge of the lake with her toe in the water. "Anyone want to swim?" she asked.

Cielle thought a swim might cool the throbbing of her foot.

"I'll go in," Cielle said, and stood. She and Trudy stripped to their bras and underpants. She didn't care. Cielle looked back and Darren sat on the sand looking their way. She wondered if he liked her body, if he thought she was pretty, and she hoped he did. Trudy wrapped her arm around Cielle's waist as they waded into the water. "He has his eyes on you," she said. "On those long skinny Jacobson legs."

When the water was up to their breasts Trudy said, "Now you can float," and she let go and swam away.

The lake was still and dark. Small bugs hovered above the water and then there was a dent of movement, a small break in the water, of life underneath coming up for air. *All of this,* Cielle thought, *all that is rising to the surface, it feels like things blooming in the dark.*

Cielle dipped below to wet her face and hair, and then lifted and floated on her back. Her ears were underwater and everything was thick with silence. She floated, weightless, and twirled herself in a circle. The last light faded from purple twilight to dark. A few stars blinked above like coins flashing in the sun. She learned in physics class that year that starlight shone down onto earth long after a star had died, and that everything and everyone was part of a star. She imagined stardust inside of her, glittering flecks of the universe, outer space swimming inside her heart and lungs and eyes. Herself and the universe expanding into nothing into something, spinning and converging, small threads pulling and connecting everything and everyone that lived and had ever lived.

She looked upside down back toward the beach. Helen stripped to her underwear and waded into the water. Around the fire there was a circle of dense and soft light; there was the smell of woodsmoke, and the popping of embers that floated up into the night. Beyond was blackness without definition.

The water rippled gently as Helen breaststroked toward her, and then Cielle felt a tug on her hand, and she lifted her head and treaded water upright. Helen was inches away, her face and hair slick and shiny in the dark.

"Everyone keeps talking about it and I don't want to talk about it," Helen said.

"Then stay out here. I'm not talking."

"Now they'll just talk about us."

"Let them talk." Cielle took water into her mouth and spit it fountainlike at Helen's face. "Float on your back and look at the stars. We're all made from stardust. Think about that."

"Mr. Bead, tenth-grade physics."

"We're just a small insignificant dot swirling around in the enormous universe."

"But nothing feels insignificant."

"No, it doesn't."

The water was warm and smooth, but Cielle's foot caught pockets of cold here and there and her flesh shivered. Those cold pockets felt like secret spaces where things got lost. They felt like quiet, empty, vast spaces, like the sky above and the water below, that sucked light and bent time. Cielle thought of the mysteries among the living — death, how the earth spun and stayed in place, the largeness of the universe, the smallness of a firefly, the miracle of life itself and that she even had a mind to think these things and ponder how the earth was held in space, and bodies of water were held in the earth — worlds in worlds and no one knew much of anything about any of them, not really.

"Make a wish on a star, Cielle. Make it a good one," Helen said.

Cielle turned and floated on her back again, and Helen did the same. Cielle straightened out her arms as if flying and she moved in the water so that the crown of her head touched Helen's. She floated, connected to her sister, weightless, darkness below and darkness above, save the distant glimmer of the stars' long-gone light reaching them. She wished for peaceful sleep-filled nights, to accept what was and would be, for unconditional love, and for no one else to leave her.

CHAPTER FIVE

The burial at Five Points Cemetery was at ten the next morning. They kept it private and small. Clouds scudded overhead in the strong breeze and whipped Cielle's hair into her eyes. Tree limbs and debris from the tornado littered the cemetery. A green mailbox was on the side of the road just outside the cemetery gates, and on it was painted OLSEN, 111 — it was Darren Olsen's address, and the house was two miles away.

Prayers and the eulogy were conducted. *We are always at the edge of a loss,* the preacher said. *Try to find acceptance in your heart, and that will lead to peace.* The cemetery was on the top of a hill, at the highest point in Boaz. Cielle saw farms and roads and hills beyond other hills. There were small lakes that looked like dark holes in the earth. In the winter, those lakes were wide-open white spaces sprinkled with ice-fishers and skaters. She wanted to know where you could look and find acceptance. She'd been praying for it. *We are tested by loss. Learn from this. From your loss come to know yourselves and your lives, know what's important; learn not what you want but what you need.* She touched the dress pocket where she carried her father's unread note. She wanted to know and didn't want to know what it said. What if his reason for wanting to die wasn't good enough? What if he didn't give a reason? What if she had more questions, and now there was no one left to answer them? There was an empty space and no one who could tell her anything that made sense.

We believe that in death, life is changed, not ended; that our life moves forward into a new fullness we can barely imagine. The Apostle Paul wrote about the change that happens to the body: we are not swallowed up by death. Our mortal body is swallowed up by life. We pass not into nothingness but into a new fullness.

Her mother did not cry. She seemed too tired, too angry to cry, and Cielle thought she deserved to be both tired and angry. Mr. Mitchell and Bodie stood on the other side of the coffin, with their arms crossed over their chests, their eyes and heads down.

85

Mrs. Mitchell sat in their car, parked just outside the cemetery gates. She said she could never watch a burial. Cielle made out her white tissue lifting up to her eyes and nose. She wondered if it was worth risking love and closeness for heartbreak and ruin. Maybe being alone was the best option; that way no one could lie to her, stop loving her, or leave her again.

There are things we cannot figure out or really understand in this life. But Lee knows now, or is beginning to know, as he comes into that eternal weight of glory beyond all measure, into the fullest presence and embrace of knowing and being known. It is this hope, this assurance, that can help us make our peace, in time, with Lee's having journeyed on now, beyond our sight, hearing, touch.

The coffin was lowered into the ground. Her mother, grandmother, sister, Mr. Mitchell, Bodie, and Cielle each shoveled dirt on it, and her mother put a white rose on top of the dirt. Her grandmother wept. Cielle and Helen held hands. Her mother stood at the edge of the grave as she used to stand on the edge of the porch watching him go as he drove off into town. Now she stood and watched him go once and for all. Cielle's chest cramped and her foot ached, and tears and noise came out of her and she couldn't stop it. He was never ever coming back.

Cielle approached the Mitchells' car and stood by the window until Mrs. Mitchell looked at her. She had bags under her eyes and a red nose. She looked down into her lap, shut her eyes, and ran her thumb over the top of her hand. Mr. Mitchell and Bodie came up behind Cielle.

"Cielle," Mr. Mitchell said. "You're welcome to come ride Ginger. You're welcome anytime."

Cielle looked at her mother standing by their truck, and she nodded yes.

"Okay," Cielle said.

Bodie hugged and kissed Helen.

"I want to go home to nap," her grandmother said.

"We'll drive you," Mr. Mitchell said.

Her grandmother rode in the back seat of the Mitchells' Oldsmobile. The car pulled away slowly, and her grandmother remained still and upright as they dipped down the hill toward the farm.

Cielle carefully walked over to the Olsens' mailbox on the side of the road, her foot still sore and aching. She bent down and looked inside. There were letters addressed in fancy cursive from Madison, Milwaukee, Ripon, and one from Minneapolis. There was an electric bill, a small package addressed to Mr. Olsen from New York City, and even a letter addressed to Darren in small, neat handwriting from Washington, D.C.

"Mom, we should take the Olsens' mailbox back to their house," Cielle said. "They have a lot of mail in there."

"Yes, Mom, because Darren might be home," Helen said.

Cielle pinched Helen's arm.

"Stop it," Helen said.

"You stop it," Cielle said.

"Cut it out," her mother said. "Let's hope their house is still standing and that everyone's all right." They loaded the mailbox onto the flatbed, and drove down County Road KK.

"It's okay to like somebody," Helen said.

"Be quiet," Cielle said.

Cielle imagined the Olsen house split apart, wooden boards scattered across the lawn, lamps and quilts in the road, a chair in a tree. If their mailbox ended up on the top of the town's hill, where might they be? The Olsens had been diary farmers, until Old Mr. Olsen bought up land after the crash. Then they had money. Darren's family moved to Chicago for years, where Mrs. Olsen went to school to become a psychologist. Then they moved back, renovated their house, and bought a new Cadillac. She'd never seen the inside of the house; her family weren't close friends of the Olsens. Even though she and Darren flirted and liked each other, they'd never officially gone on a date.

They coasted into the valley, where trees thinned out and gave way to fields. Green to yellow-brown. A jagged line cut through the edge of the Olsens' cornfield as if a truck had rammed through at full speed for hundreds of yards. The ground was churned into a deep dark furrow.

"That's where the funnel ran." Cielle pointed.

Helen leaned forward. "Oh, my God."

It was hard to say where the funnel started. There was a fresh hole in the ground by the road where the mailbox had been sucked out and flung away. The car turned onto the Olsens' driveway. Cielle's heart rushed. The house came into view, intact and white as a bone, with the hanging baskets of lobelia, the delicate purple flowers untouched and dangling perfectly from the porch.

"Okay, good," her mother said. "Very

good." She patted Cielle's thigh. "Very good."

A curtain parted in a downstairs window but she couldn't tell who was looking out at them.

"Well, let's get their mailbox back to them," Cielle's mother said. "Whether they come out to greet us or not."

Helen and Cielle pulled the mailbox from the flatbed. The long, square wooden base was heavy. They each took an end and walked toward the porch.

Cielle's mother leaned out her window. "Prop it up against the rail there," she said, "and easy on that foot, Cielle." They righted the post and made sure the mailbox opening faced outward.

Cielle looked back into the mailbox. She liked the look of the script on the letters. They hardly ever got mail from anyone other than relatives for birthdays or Christmas.

Helen looked at her hands, brown with dirt, and raised the red flag on the mailbox. "Go knock on the door, Cielle. I want to see inside."

The curtains to the right of the porch pulled back again. Cielle waved and the curtains quickly fell shut.

"Go knock." Helen pushed Cielle toward

the steps.

Cielle stumbled up the stairs, wiped a line of dirt from her black dress, and knocked on the front door. There was rustling and footsteps, and a woman's voice from the other side of the door said, "Oh, hell."

Cielle looked back at Helen and raised her shoulders.

"Is that you, Mrs. Olsen?" Cielle asked.

"This is Mrs. Olsen."

"This is Cielle Jacobson, Mrs. Olsen. We found your mailbox on the side of the road by Five Points Cemetery."

"I know who you are," she said. There was the metal click of a lock, and the door opened a crack. Mrs. Olsen hid her body behind the door and all Cielle saw were her eyes, bloodshot and as dark as night. "I know who you are, Miss Cielle. I've seen you play your violin in the school concert."

"You have mail in there," Cielle said. She had never spoken to or seen Mrs. Olsen up close before yesterday. She'd only seen her from afar in the supermarket, or while she waited for Darren in her Cadillac outside of school. Cielle smelled scrambled eggs and brewed coffee and cigarette smoke.

Mrs. Olsen's hand wrapped around the edge of the door. Her nails were long and shiny; she had a French manicure. "You

91

play the violin very well," she said. The lapel of her silken ruby robe fluttered in the wind.

"Thank you," Cielle said. She wanted to touch Mrs. Olsen's fingernails. They were perfect.

"The violin is my favorite instrument." Mrs. Olsen sniffled and wiped the edge of her eye. She wasn't crying, but her eyes leaked. She reached out and touched the wooden bird pin Cielle wore on her dress. She traced the wing.

"Isn't that pretty," Mrs. Olsen said. "That's lovely."

"My father made it," Cielle said.

Helen came up behind Cielle and leaned her head toward the crack to see Mrs. Olsen. Mrs. Olsen startled, drew her arm back, and held her robe together at her chest.

"I'm sorry about your father, girls."

"I'm Helen Jacobson, Mrs. Olsen. You have a lovely home."

Cielle held her dress down at her sides so the wind wouldn't blow it up. "She's my older sister."

"We found your mailbox, Cielle found it, on the side of the road outside the cemetery," Helen said.

"We don't go to church," Mrs. Olsen said. "So thank you for finding it."

Helen stood on her tiptoes and leaned in for more of a look. "We just had our father's burial."

"I'm sorry," she said. "I'm very sorry."

"If you ever need someone to watch your house while you're gone . . ." Helen said, and stood up straight, as if she were interviewing for a job. "I'm going to Madison for college, but I'll come back to take care of it."

"She wants to see what your house looks like inside," Cielle said.

A phlegm-filled cough came from the kitchen, a smoker's cough. He coughed deep in his throat over and over, cleared his throat, and spit. Mrs. Olsen leaned her face into the crack between the door and the frame, and a tear leaked out of her left eye. She didn't bother wiping it away and it trailed down her cheek. "Come over another day, girls," she said. "Your mother's waiting." She tapped her fingernails on the door, waved to their mother in the truck, and then shut the door.

Cielle's mother pulled back onto County Road KK. "What did she say?"

"That the violin is her favorite instrument," Cielle said.

"She seems flighty," her mother said.

"She seems nice, but sad," Cielle said.

93

"What's there to be sad about with a house like that?" Helen asked.

"Everyone has something to be sad about," Cielle's mother said. "Don't ever forget that."

Cielle knew that was true, but thought it might be easier to recover from sadness if you didn't have to worry about money or losing your home and farm, that maybe then your loss felt like a sting rather than a long, dark tunnel with no end in sight.

Her mother passed the road to their house and headed toward Richland Center. "I don't feel like going home and looking at that mess of a barn and tiptoeing around while your grandmother sleeps. Let's do something nice after this awful week. How about Sunday brunch?"

"An omelet," Cielle said. "A strawberry tart."

"French toast with extra maple syrup," Helen said. "Bacon and pineapple juice."

"Now we're talking," her mother said. "And waffles, sausage, coffee, and chocolate cake."

She parked in front of the Bredahl Inn on Main Street, where inside there were pretty patterned Oriental rugs and high ceilings with ornate molding and chandeliers. "We could eat here more often if we lived in

94

town," her mother said.

"You can't leave the farm," Helen said. "We can't move."

"You hate the farm," Cielle said. "What do you care?"

They slid out of the truck. Nothing in town looked touched by the tornado. Pots full of deep purple and yellow pansies lined the inn's porch. Pleated and fanned American flags draped from the railing, not one out of place. Colorfully illustrated war effort posters that read ARE YOU DOING ALL THAT YOU CAN?, and DO WITH LESS SO THEY'LL HAVE ENOUGH, and WE HAVE JUST BEGUN TO FIGHT! hung from lampposts and in windows. Helen walked ahead of them and stood in front of the inn's door, her arms folded tightly across her chest.

"Mother, are you going to sell the farm?" Helen asked.

"You want to discuss this right now?" Her mother raised her eyebrows.

"Will I have a place to come home to at Christmas?"

"You will have someplace to come home to, but I can't promise you it will be the farm."

Helen widened her stance. "You can't sell the farm."

"It's not mine to sell, honey. Mr. Olsen

95

owns it."

"What is it with you?" Cielle said. "You've been yammering nonstop about how you'll never live on a farm again and how you can't wait to go to college."

Her mother put her hands on Helen's shoulders and moved her to the side of the door to let people walk out of the inn. The smell of breakfast wafted out — coffee, eggs, cooked meats, and pastries. Her mother pulled Helen into her so they were almost nose-to-nose. "Our options are limited," her mother said softly. "With the barn gone, and your father gone, we might not have a choice. Things are different now."

"Too many things," Helen said.

"You're leaving," Cielle said.

"I could stay," Helen said. "Maybe I should."

Her mother bit her bottom lip, and then walked past Helen, inside. Cielle didn't know if her mother wanted Helen to stay but wouldn't say it, or didn't want her to stay. She couldn't tell.

Helen looked at Cielle. "I could stay and help."

"What would you do that for?" Cielle asked.

The Bredahl Inn was crowded with the

after-church crowd. Glasses and plates were clinked and scraped, waiters scurried, floral and spicy perfumes lingered in the air. Vases with white and yellow roses sat on the tables. They ordered and sat quietly.

"We haven't eaten out in a long time." Cielle's mother flapped open her linen napkin and smoothed it over her lap. "It's nice to see people."

"Do you recognize anyone?" Cielle asked.

Helen craned her neck. "The Sullivans, in the corner."

The waiter delivered their juices and a coffee for Cielle's mother. Then came waffles with strawberries and whipped cream and sausage for Cielle's mother, an omelet with bacon and toast for Cielle and French toast with maple syrup, bacon, and roasted potatoes for Helen.

"Bon appétit," the waiter said.

"Merci," Cielle said.

"Listen to you," Helen said. "Well done."

"Thank you for treating us today, Mother," Cielle said.

"Yes, thank you, Mother," Helen said.

Cielle's mother extended her arms to the girls, and they all held hands. "I love you both. Let's be thankful for each other, and for the time we had with your father." Her mother bowed her head and Helen bowed hers as well. Cielle kept hers up, her eyes open, and watched her mother and Helen, looked at their hands that linked them together. How did people forgive and move on? What mattered and kept anyone caring about what they did, how they did it, or with whom they did it if in the end they would die and it would all be over, gone, forgotten, dark, dust in the ground, a name on a headstone?

"Helen," her mother said. "We need to start thinking about what you'll need in Madison. What you want to take from home for your dormitory room."

"Mom," Helen said, "I —" She breathed in and then coughed, and her eyes widened. She held her hand to her throat and waved her other hand in front of her face as if she were hot and needed to be cooled.

"She's choking. Are you choking?" Cielle asked.

Helen nodded yes. Helen tried to force air, tried to push out what was caught in her throat. Her face reddened and was close to maroon.

Cielle's mother stood fast and knocked over her chair. She slapped Helen on the back. "Somebody help," she said.

Cielle felt every inch of her body, but didn't know which way to move. Her mother made a fist and hit Helen's back so hard it sounded like a deep drum. The room quieted and people sat still at their tables. It was a summer brunch crowd of butter-yellows, sea-foam-greens, charcoal-grays, and poppy-reds.

Cielle stood and nudged her mother aside. She reached her arms around Helen, who was wheezing and a shade darker, close to violet. She once saw someone punch a choking person's stomach, which made the food come up. She made a fist under her sister's rib cage and pulled as hard as she could. She felt the softness of Helen's middle, the bone of her rib cage, the density of her insides. But her sister was still choking.

"Why don't you people do something?" her mother yelled.

A waiter in a bow tie ran out from the kitchen. Cielle stepped aside when she saw him rushing toward their table. He steadied himself behind Helen. "What's her name?" he asked.

"Helen," Cielle said. The waiter had frosting on his hand and smelled like butter cake.

"Here we go, Helen," he said. In one motion he pressed the palm of his hand into her stomach and hit her back, and a piece of potato came up. It flew out of her mouth and landed in her juice glass. The crowd clapped. The waiter rubbed Helen's upper arms and leaned toward her ear. "Okay?"

Helen gasped and her breaths were rough. She touched his hand on her arm and then her chin bunched and she cried. She shook and cried and her red face was wet with tears. The waiter stayed close, his hands on her arms. "You're okay," he said, and pointed to the glass of juice. "That was a nice shot."

Helen laughed and the crowd clapped again. Cielle heard whispered words: *Of all days, their father, poor things,* and *Can you imagine?*

Everyone had turned toward them with crooked smiles, soft eyes, heads shaking back and forth, hands clasped. Cielle felt the way she had in anxious dreams — late someplace and standing naked in the middle of a room full of strangers, lost.

CHAPTER SIX

That week they went about their chores of collecting eggs, feeding animals, cleaning pens, and milking cows. The hay needed to be cut and baled. The mess of the barn had to be cleaned up and cleared away. Cielle still had her father's note folded up in her pocket.

On Friday, before school, Cielle watered and weeded the garden while it was still cool outside. She picked whatever was vine-ripe for later: zucchini and yellow beans, tomatoes and beets. She dressed for school and looked at the note. She unfolded it and left it right-side down. She could see it wasn't long, and it seemed too few words to explain everything. She wasn't ready, so she folded it back up and carried it in her pocket for the time when she felt ready. She told herself any normal person would read the note and move on. If she wanted the truth so badly, there it was, and all she needed to do was look at it. But she didn't. She wondered if she was like her mother and Helen. Maybe to survive you had to be able to look beyond ugly, dark things in the world, even if it meant pretending. Maybe the people who could do that were the happy ones.

That afternoon, Cielle walked home from summer school and as she neared the turn for Kanton Street she heard Bodie yell her name out from behind. She turned and Bodie nodded and jogged to catch up. A corridor of late-day sunlight shone out in front of him like an aisle of gold.

"Afternoon," she said.

"It is," he said, "and hot." He threw a peach up and caught it behind his back.

"Show-off," Cielle said. He bit into the peach. Juice dripped and he wiped his chin on his shirtsleeve. His hair lightened every summer and it was close to white, and curled around his ears and at the base of his neck. He was strong, and lines of muscle defined his forearms like small gullies. He had graduated with Helen, but had to finish classes with tutors from his four weeks out in February with the measles. Cielle thought of Helen running her hands over his arms, or his arms wrapped around Helen, and she thought of Darren and it gave her goose bumps.

"You're walking better," he said.

"My foot's an awful shade of yellow and green, but the hurt is gone," she said.

They walked the dirt road, and cornstalks stood a foot away. Cielle yanked an ear of sweet corn from one of the yellowing stalks.

"It might not taste right," Bodie said.

"We'll see." Cielle shucked the casing and picked the fine silk from the corn. The kernels were light yellow and not as plump and full as they should be, but when she bit in, it was still sweet.

"It's good enough," she said. She didn't know why anyone cooked corn when it was delicious raw.

"Summer school's over," Cielle said.

"It's over," Bodie said. "And that's the last time I'll ever think about chemistry. You want to cut over the hill?"

Cielle's house was two miles one-way from school, but there was a shortcut up a steep wooded hill that went through the Gundersons' farm.

"Not today," Cielle said. "Not in this dress." The wooded section had blackberry brambles and she didn't want to snag the fine cotton of her sundress on a thorn.

He dropped the peach pit and kicked it. It

spun through the air and hit a tree with a loud crack.

"Are you and Helen going to the lake?" Cielle asked.

"I thought I'd stop by to see her. Helen said you're going to the fair tonight with Darren Olsen?"

Cielle felt the heat in her face, and ate her corn.

"I like Darren," Bodie said.

"I like the Ferris wheel ride."

"That's a good ride," he said. "Darren is nice too." Bodie poked his finger into her shoulder.

"You're annoying."

He poked her again and she raised the corncob at him.

"Cielle Jacobson," Bodie said. "Little Cielle Jacobson." He swiped her corncob, threw it far into the field, and put his arm around her shoulders.

They walked down the road as it sloped and curved to the right toward her house. His arm kept her tucked into his side, and she felt safe there.

"I need you to show me how to cut and bale the fields," Cielle said. "We need help with the farm."

"I can help you," he said.

Her father had told her to never expect

anything from anyone, and that if you asked favors you had to be prepared to return favors, but that it wasn't good to owe anything to anyone. Keeping people at a distance in that way seemed harsh and unnecessary to her. She believed people wanted connection, and wanted to be relied on and be reliable when needed. She hardly asked for help, but it felt good to ask Bodie for help.

"I don't know what to say about your dad. I don't want you to think I'm avoiding it," Bodie said.

"You don't have to say anything."

If she read the note, then maybe there'd be something to say, but there was nothing she or anyone could change. She kept it in her pocket during the day and under her pillow at night because writing it was one of the last things her father had done while he was alive. The note was like those unopened letters in Darren Olsen's mailbox; it held the possibility of news yet to come. They were words, good or bad, her father had not yet spoken to her. She was afraid to read it — afraid they'd be words she didn't want to read and remember him by.

Bodie cleared his throat. Cielle matched her stride with his so their steps moved in unison. His hand was rough and callused

105

on her shoulder. He cleared his throat again.

"I joined the Army Air Corps," he said. "Last November, when I'd just turned eighteen. Training was deferred until school ended, and my letter came a week ago."

Cielle stopped and moved from under his arm.

He looked at the ground. "They train in Texas. I leave in a few weeks."

"You're serious?"

"I want to serve. I've always wanted to fly."

"I hate this war."

"Helen's not going to understand. She wants to get engaged."

"So get engaged."

He turned and looked into the cornfield and kept his back to her. "But what if I don't come back?"

"I thought you wanted to marry Helen."

"I do, but I don't know if I should." He kicked the road with the toe of his shoe. "I don't know what to do."

"My mother said if boys aren't saying yes, then they're saying no."

He turned back and looked at her. His eyelids seemed heavy and tired from turning these thoughts over and over. "It's not that simple. I don't have a job, I have no money, and I might be gone for a year or longer, or dead. It feels unfair to ask her to wait."

Her adrenaline spiked at the word *dead.* She bit her bottom lip.

"I'm sorry to say that word," Bodie said.

She couldn't look at him. Couldn't imagine him *dead.* She was still working out what dead meant: gone, erased, nothing, invisible, nowhere, forever.

"What I mean is that it's complicated," Bodie said.

"It's simple," Cielle said. "You're making it complicated."

Bodie walked ahead and she walked behind him.

"If you've changed your mind about Helen that's fine, but don't make excuses."

He walked slowly and looked up at the sky as though he might find an answer there. She looked up too. The sky was a deep royal blue, a wide summer sky. A breeze rustled the leaves of the trees and sent a flock of starlings out into the air. They dipped into a dive, and rose up and over the trees. She wondered what it felt like to fly and sail and soar through air, among and into the blue. *And when boys are quiet like now, it's because you've said something true they don't want to admit,* she thought.

"There are too many people dying," she said.

"Everyone enlisted or is getting called up. Billy, Nathan, James. Joe Downs even signed up."

"I don't care."

Bodie shook his head back and forth and walked ahead. "Most people think this is the right thing to do."

"I'm not most people."

"You think I'm doing the wrong thing?"

"I can't stand the thought of you not coming back."

She'd never known this one thing so clearly before: people leave. No matter how many times she asked someone to stay, no matter how desperately she wanted them to stay, there was a revolving door, and people came and went. Sometimes it had something to do with her, but mostly it had nothing to do with her. The universe was in constant motion. Her own molecules and atoms were vibrating and colliding. The human heart pumped blood throughout the body. Continents drifted across the surface of the planet, and the earth spun day and night. The universe stretched and expanded, and, according to Hubble's law, galaxies receded from each other. As did people — they came together and moved away. They

108

never stopped moving.

"You need to tell Helen. I'm not telling her," Cielle said.

They walked. Cornstalks shuffled in the wind, so dry they sounded like paper. A tractor motor hummed in the distance. She'd known Bodie since she was born. His shoulder blades moved under his shirt as he walked. His arms and neck were tan and smooth. *We're alive,* she thought, *and it's a miraculous thing.* She didn't want her world to keep shifting. She knew even if he survived the war, he might not come back to Boaz or he'd come back a different person, and Helen herself might not come back. The life she knew now wouldn't exist. It would be gone, with just a few artifacts left behind as proof it once existed.

A black Chevrolet sedan passed, then stopped and backed up toward them.

"Who's that?" Cielle said.

"I don't know." Bodie stood in front of Cielle. "But he's not smart to back up on this road."

The waiter from the Bredahl Inn leaned out his window. "You're Helen's sister, from Sunday, right?"

"I'm Helen's sister from Sunday," Cielle said.

"She left her shawl at the restaurant," he

said. "I was headed to your house to drop it off. You all want a ride?"

The waiter held out his hand to Bodie. "I'm Matthew Vorland. I work at the Bredahl Inn."

"Bodie Mitchell, Helen's boyfriend." They shook hands. "This is Cielle, Helen's sister from Sunday."

Matthew shook Cielle's hand. "It's hot as hell, get in the car," he said.

Bodie went to the front passenger's seat and Cielle got in the back.

"We're not far," Cielle said. "Next farm on the right, about a mile."

Matthew nodded. His car was clean. No dirt, no wrappers, no nothing. The back of his neck beaded with sweat. Helen's light blue shawl was on the front seat between Matthew and Bodie. It lifted and fluttered from the wind. Bodie picked it up and held it on his lap.

"I've never seen you before," Bodie said. "Is your family from around here?"

"From Chicago, but my sister married one of the Bredahl boys and they gave me a temporary job at the inn. What do you all do around here?"

"I'm almost sixteen and still in school."

Matthew looked at Cielle in the rearview mirror. "Almost sweet sixteen," he said, and winked. "And you, Bodie?"

"Enlisted. Army Air Corps."

"Brave," Matthew said.

"You're not enlisting?" Bodie asked.

"Can't," he said, "bum knees and asthma."

"Helen will be going to college in Madison," Bodie said.

"Maybe," Cielle said.

"What do you mean, maybe?" Bodie turned in his seat.

The mailbox was up ahead. "That's our driveway." Cielle leaned forward and pointed. Bodie raised his eyebrows and Cielle raised her eyebrows back at him.

"Does Helen feel all right?" Matthew asked.

"From choking on a potato? She's fine," Bodie said.

"She was upset," Matthew said.

"Her father just died," Bodie said. "Of course she was upset."

"She's all right," Cielle said. "It just scared her."

"That seems natural." Matthew slowly turned into the driveway and parked.

"You're a waiter," Bodie said, "and a psychologist?"

Matthew turned and smiled at Bodie. "I'm just returning her shawl," he said.

Bodie picked up the shawl and lifted it in

the air like a drink. "Yes, you are."

"Be safe and come home alive." Matthew held out his hand to shake, but Bodie turned and stepped out of the car.

"Don't worry about me," Bodie said, and walked toward the house.

There were five men cutting and loading what was left of the barn's wood onto the flatbed of a large truck. The boards were splintered and long. Dust hovered and floated in the low afternoon sunlight.

Cielle got out and leaned down toward Matthew's window. "I'm sorry."

"You've got nothing to be sorry for."

"Thank you," she said, even though she felt sorry for all sorts of things.

"What happened to your barn?"

"Tornado."

"You've had a hell of a summer."

"Bodie's a nice person, just confused right now." Cielle looked toward the house. She adjusted her satchel and cradled her violin case in her arms.

"Forget about Bodie."

"You seem smart to me. Too smart for a waiter."

"I'm waiting tables while I study for the bar exam." He squinted up at her and tapped the car door.

"To work in a bar?" Cielle asked.

Matthew laughed. He had straight, white teeth. "To practice as an attorney," he said, "although I wouldn't mind learning how to mix a few drinks."

Matthew looked beyond Cielle and waved. Cielle turned, and Helen stood at the screen door inside the kitchen with her shawl.

"She better go to college," Cielle said.

Wooden boards boomed as they were dropped onto the truck's flatbed.

"We all end up where we're supposed to somehow." Matthew tapped the side of the door again. "Take care, Cielle, almost sweet sixteen," he said, and shifted the car into reverse. "I'll see you around." He slowly backed out of the driveway.

Cielle stood by the screen door and listened to Bodie and Helen bickering inside.

"I see you, Cielle," Helen said. "You told Bodie I might not go to college?"

"Why wouldn't you go?" Bodie asked Helen.

Bodie's footsteps paced the kitchen.

"Cielle, get in here," Helen yelled.

Cielle walked in. "I didn't do anything," she said, and put her satchel and violin case on the kitchen table.

"You two. I can do whatever I want." Helen pointed at her own chest.

"Do you want to stay here for Matthew?" Bodie asked.

"Who?" Helen said.

"The waiter who saved you," Cielle said. "His name is Matthew."

"I didn't even know his name. What does he have to do with this?"

"It's obvious he likes you," Bodie said.

"He saved my life and returned my shawl, give him a little credit," Helen said. "Don't turn this around. If I decide to stay home for a year to help my mother with our farm, then I will." She bit her lower lip, threw her shawl at Bodie, and went upstairs.

Cielle raised her eyebrows.

"I don't want to hear it, Cielle, I already know what you think," Bodie said. He handed the shawl to her on his way out the door.

"Bodie, the hay," Cielle said.

"Not today." Bodie walked into the field to go through the woods to his house. On the way, Cielle saw him pick the grass and survey the field from all sides as her father had done. She knew it was ready to cut and bale.

Her grandmother came up from the cellar and peeked from around the door. "That was a commotion," she said.

"I know it," Cielle said.

Her grandmother carried a wooden crate full of canned preserves.

Cielle put her satchel and violin case by the door and noticed her father's work boots on the floor, unlaced and caked with dirt as if he'd just taken them off.

"Were those there before?" Cielle pointed at the boots.

"I imagine so."

"Where are you putting those jars?" Cielle asked.

"Might try to sell them at the farmers' market. It might be a way for your mother to make pocket money. She's good with canning and pickling."

Cielle saw her father's green coffee mug on top of the icebox. She took it down, and there was half a cup of cold coffee in it. She set it back.

"Hand that over, and I'll wash it," her grandmother said.

"Leave it," Cielle said.

"It can't sit there forever." Her grandmother reached for the cup and looked into it. "There's coffee in here."

"Put it back," Cielle said.

"Cielle, sweetheart."

"Put it back."

"There are all sorts of things we're going to have to sort through."

Cielle took the mug from her grandmother. "Don't touch anything, don't move anything, don't throw anything away." Cielle put the mug back on top of the icebox.

Upstairs, Cielle washed her face and the cold water felt good. Her father's razor sat on the edge of the sink in the bathroom, dark hairs still on the porcelain underneath the blade. Her face was red from the heat, red as an apple, so she wet a towel and went into her bedroom, lay on her bed, and placed the cold towel on her forehead.

"I just want to be normal," she said softly. "I want life to be normal." Cielle's limbs loosened and her back settled into the mattress. She heard footsteps.

"Too late for that," Helen said.

Cielle tilted her head and looked at Helen from the corner of her eye.

Helen lay down on her stomach, propped up on her elbows. "If you were me, what would you do?"

"What are your choices?"

"Madison or home."

"I wouldn't give up what was important to me. I would go to Madison."

"You're important. Bodie's important. The farm's important."

"Don't stay home. You'll get stuck here," Cielle said.

Helen turned onto her back and pulled her knees to her chest. She took Cielle's towel and put it on her own forehead. "I'm afraid of making the wrong choice."

"You won't make the wrong choice."

"You don't know that."

"Fear isn't a good reason to do or not do something."

"I'm not afraid."

"Sounds like you're afraid of what you don't know, and you're thinking of staying home because it's what you do know."

Helen bit her pinkie finger and her eyes watered. She kicked the bed with her legs. "I don't want to talk about it."

"I'm not going to make you."

"What are you going to wear to the fair tonight?" she asked.

"My yellow sundress."

"Get dressed, then."

Cielle dressed and then Helen knelt on the bed behind her and brushed her hair. The brush on her scalp and Helen's hands on the base of her neck and around her ears made Cielle want to fall asleep sitting up.

"It's so hot; you should wear your hair up." Helen brushed Cielle's hair up into a ponytail. Then she dabbed on some of her jasmine perfume behind Cielle's ears and smudged berry-colored lipstick on her lips.

It was close to five o'clock, and the summer sun had hours before setting. Cielle sat on the couch by the window and waited for Darren while her mother, grandmother, and Helen ate at the table. At six o'clock, Darren still hadn't shown. The table was cleared and the dishes cleaned and put away. Her mother and grandmother sat in chairs across from her, resewing buttons onto a dress and needlepointing.

"Maybe he thought you were meeting another night," her mother said.

"I doubt it."

"Maybe something happened at home and the phone line was tied up."

Cielle's upper lip beaded with sweat and she wiped it with her dress strap.

"That's ladylike," her mother said.

"Who cares?" Cielle said. "We need to cut and bale hay this week."

"I'll call Jim."

"I want to do it."

"It's too dangerous for a girl." Her mother's fingers nimbly wove thread through buttonholes.

"She could do it, Olive," her grandmother said. "There's nothing too dangerous for a girl."

"I don't need my daughter mangled by a tractor."

"We'll do it together. We'll clean up those fields." Her grandmother clicked her needles together. "You need to teach these girls how to take care of things and how to take care of themselves."

"How long are you staying?" her mother asked.

"I'm staying until I know things are running smoothly around here," her grandmother said.

"Don't you have somewhere you need to be?"

"I haven't needed to be anywhere my whole life," she said. "I choose to be where I am, and right now that's here."

"Might someone need you somewhere else?"

"We're family," she said.

Helen walked downstairs wearing a cornflower-blue sundress with her hair curled.

"Look at you," her mother said. "You have a date too?"

Helen took Cielle's hand and pulled her up from the couch. "We're going to the fair."

Cielle groaned and rolled her eyes. "You don't have to."

"We're dressed. Get your things and get in the truck." Helen straightened the strap of Cielle's dress and patted her on the butt.

"Let's go."

Helen backed out of the driveway. What was left of the barn's wood was neatly stacked for the men to pick up and haul away the next day, and then all that would be left was the foundation. The house was dark except for a string of low sunlight that shone into the living room where her mother and grandmother sat in chairs quietly working their fingers over cloth, her mother mending something old, and her grandmother creating a picture of something new.

The Olsens' mailbox had been put back out and Helen pulled onto the grassy shoulder of the road right in front of it.

"Helen, please don't do this," Cielle said.

"Let's go see what happened here," Helen said.

"Nothing happened. Don't embarrass me."

"It's rude to stand people up and keep them waiting." Helen slid out of the truck and walked to the mailbox, where the red flag was up. "Mrs. Olsen told us to come back. Relax." She opened the mailbox lid. Cielle walked up beside her. There was one letter sitting in there. Helen looked at Cielle and smiled. "Take it," Helen said.

"You take it," Cielle said.

Helen reached for the letter. "Christian Olsen. Washington, D.C. Who lives there?"

"Christian Olsen."

"Who's he?"

"A relative?"

"I'm short-fused tonight." Helen lifted the skirt of her dress and tucked the letter into the back of her underwear.

"What's wrong with you?"

"I'm sick of liars and people who hide the truth." She adjusted and straightened her dress.

"So you steal their letters? I can tell you have something under your dress."

Helen ran her hand over her lower back to feel for the envelope and shrugged her shoulders. "You stole a letter," she said, and walked toward the Olsens' house. Lights were on inside. This time the curtains weren't shut and the front door was open.

"What letter?"

"The one Mom had the night of the tornado."

Cielle shut the mailbox lid and lowered the red flag and walked behind Helen. "She's our mother. The Olsens have nothing to do with us."

"What did it say?"

"I don't know. I haven't read it." She touched her dress pockets, but she'd left the note under her pillow at home.

Small green flickers of fireflies appeared over the lawn and at the edge of the woods. Cielle thought of them as night spirits, angels glowing in the dark. The gravel driveway crunched under their shoes and Helen walked straight up the front steps and knocked on the screen door. There was a large wooden table with a porcelain vase on it in the hall, and Oriental rugs in ruby-reds and burnt-oranges covered shiny dark wood floors. Bookcases lined the walls in the living room to the right.

Helen bit her thumb. "If you're keeping something from me, Lucille Patricia Jacobson, then I'd like you to think long and hard about how to tell me what it is you might know."

"I know an awful lot you don't know, Helen Camilla Jacobson, and I'm not sure you want to know what I know."

"Intriguing," Helen said. "I want to know."

Voices came from another room, but no one came to the door. Cielle thought Helen might want to know, but would regret the knowing once she was told.

Helen knocked again and in a loud sing-songy voice said, "Hello?"

"Don't make a scene," Cielle said.

The chatter paused and the clacking of

heels came around the corner. Mrs. Olsen wore a baby-blue linen dress and baby-blue high heels. Her hair was swept up into a neat twist, not a hair out of place. Her mouth was painted in velvety red lipstick and looked like a rose petal. She carried a drink in one hand and a cigarette in the other.

"The Jacobson girls!" she said, as if they were invited guests. "Open that screen door, my hands are full."

Helen pulled open the door and stepped into the foyer. Mrs. Olsen leaned in and pecked each of them on the cheek and stepped back. "Look at you two, what lovely summer dresses." She teetered backward and righted herself with a wider stance.

"Sorry to interrupt your party," Cielle said.

"Nonsense." Mrs. Olsen stepped toward the vase and tapped her cigarette ash inside of it. She smiled at Cielle and Helen; her cheeks were flushed and her eyes were glassy.

"Is Darren home?" Helen asked.

"Darren?" Mrs. Olsen creased her forehead. She seemed not to recognize her own son's name. "He's somewhere. I don't know where. Maybe you want something to drink, girls? You're old enough to drink." Mrs.

Olsen walked back toward the kitchen and the voices.

"Why not?" Helen said, and took Cielle's hand.

"Why not is right," Mrs. Olsen said. "We have mixed nuts and pickled vegetables, cheese and crackers, so help yourselves. You're both so skinny. Eat something. Eat some protein."

Another couple her parents' age whom she didn't recognize, and a man Cielle assumed to be Mr. Olsen, sat in the living room and watched Cielle and Helen.

"These are the Jacobson girls, dear," Mrs. Olsen said. She put ice in two tumblers and poured whiskey over the top. Mrs. Olsen handed the drinks to Helen and then Cielle. Cielle had never drunk whiskey before, and the smell burned her nose. No one said anything, but Cielle saw recognition in their faces at the mention of their last name. They all seemed to inhale deeply with regret. Cielle knew that if they knew her father, then they knew how old she and Helen were, but no one made a fuss about the drinks. Mr. Olsen had a handful of nuts, and placed them in his mouth all at once.

"I'm Andrew Olsen and this is John and Judy Schmitt," he said. Cielle had heard the name Schmitt. They had children who were older, already in college and married.

Mr. Schmitt raised his glass and said, "To your health, girls." They all raised a glass and leaned over to clink Helen and Cielle's glasses before drinking. Cielle sipped the whiskey, and it was hot and burned from her mouth down to her gut.

Mrs. Olsen sat on Mr. Olsen's lap, wobbled on his thigh, and almost fell over. He took her arm and put it around his neck. "You should hear Cielle play the violin," she said, "she's a real talent." Mrs. Olsen smiled and looked right at Cielle, but Cielle didn't think she could see straight. Water leaked from her left eye again.

"How about that?" Mrs. Schmitt said. "I never could read music." She put her hand on her husband's arm, and when he looked at her she raised her eyebrows. Cielle knew that look. Her mother used to give it to her father when it was time to leave.

"Cielle, Cielle." Mrs. Olsen stood and hurried around the corner. "Hold on, Cielle, hold on," she said. She heard a door open and objects being shoved and pushed around in a closet.

"Mr. Olsen." Helen leaned forward in her chair. "Where is Darren?"

"Darren?"

"He was supposed to meet Cielle at our

house earlier to go to the fair."

Mrs. Schmitt put her hand on her chest. "Darren is such a nice boy. How is he doing?"

No one said anything. Cielle put her drink on the coffee table.

"You don't like whiskey?" Mr. Olsen asked.

"I don't think so," Cielle said. Mr. Olsen picked up her glass and poured it into his own.

"I don't much care for whiskey either." He took a sharp shot of the drink and then he stood. "Darling, for the love of God, what are you doing out there?"

Mrs. Olsen scurried around the corner holding a violin case. "I found it. I thought Cielle could play for us." She held the violin out toward Cielle.

"I don't think that's a good idea," Mr. Olsen said. "The girls are on their way to the fair."

"Cielle is very good," Helen said.

Mr. Olsen moved toward Mrs. Olsen. "Don't put Cielle on the spot. Give me the violin." He took the case from her. "The girls are supposed to meet Darren."

Mrs. Schmitt winked at Cielle. "Darren is such a handsome boy."

Mrs. Olsen lit a cigarette. "My older son

126

played the violin like an angel."

Helen ran her hand over her dress and sat back. "I didn't know you had another son," she said.

Mrs. Olsen looked at Mr. Olsen. She took a long drag on her cigarette and exhaled smoke. "It's funny, the things you don't know about your own neighbors, isn't it?"

"Or your own parents," Cielle said.

Mrs. Olsen nodded her head up and down, agreeing with Cielle. "I know, honey." Mrs. Olsen wiped the wet from under her eye. "We all have secrets. Children don't get to know certain things about their parents."

"We're not children," Cielle said. "I'm not a child."

"You're somebody's child." Mrs. Olsen leaned down and took off her heels. "You'll always be somebody's child." She set her shoes next to the chair and wiggled her toes.

"My daughters will always be my babies," Mrs. Schmitt said. "It's true."

"You miss your children when they leave," Mrs. Olsen said.

Cielle looked at Mrs. Olsen. "I'm sorry about your son. Darren said he passed away."

Mrs. Schmitt gasped. "He did?"

"He did not," Mrs. Olsen said softly.

Mr. Olsen took a few steps back into the

room. "Girls, I'll be sure to tell Darren you came by." He extended his arm toward the front door.

Helen drank the last of her whiskey and stood.

"Christian did not die," Mrs. Olsen said. "That's not true."

"I'm sorry," Cielle said, and stood to follow Helen.

"Why would Darren say that?" Mrs. Olsen asked.

"To make me feel better," Cielle said.

Helen squeezed her hand. "Come on, Cielle."

"How does saying someone's dead who's not make anyone feel better?" Mrs. Olsen's lip tugged up at the edge of her mouth. "Did that make you feel better?"

Helen pulled Cielle toward the door. Mrs. Olsen followed them with her drink in hand.

"Wait," she said. Mrs. Olsen stood between them and the door. "Tell me if that news made you feel better. I'd like to know. My heart is pounding so hard, I don't know what I think. My head is in another universe. Did his telling you his brother died make you feel better?" Her whiskey sloshed around in the glass and an ice cube popped out and slid across the wood floor right in front of Cielle.

"Yes," Cielle said, and she dragged the toe of her shoe through the wet on the floor and then looked up. "It did. It made me feel less alone."

Mrs. Olsen had one hand on her hip and her lips were parted, but no sound came out of her mouth.

"Good night," Mr. Olsen said. He opened the screen door and they walked back to their truck in the dark.

Helen stopped at the mailbox, lifted her dress, and put the letter to Christian Olsen back inside and raised the red flag.

At the fair, bright lights spun against the night sky. Smells of barbecued meat, fried dough, and beer wafted through the air, and tinny horn music wailed around every corner. Cielle passed a mirror and her body looked stretched lengthwise, like a piece of taffy pulled long and thin. The Ferris wheel turned and turned, with its chairs rocking back and forth.

Helen moved toward the baseball stand. "Let's throw things," she said. "That will make me feel better." She paid a man three cents for three baseballs, aimed at the bottles on the platform, and missed all three.

"Your turn," Helen said, and paid three

more cents and handed Cielle three base-balls. Cielle focused on the bottle, wound her arm back, and threw hard. She knocked a bottle off the stand.

"Down she goes!" the man yelled.

She felt powerful. A force snaked through her arm and she knocked over two more bottles.

"Pick your prize! Pick your prize!" the man bellowed.

Cielle didn't want to carry around a bulky stuffed animal, so she pointed to a silver key chain dangling from a hook that had a metal pendant on it that read *Wisconsin* in curving red letters. The man handed it to her. She twirled the key ring around her finger and she and Helen walked among the stalls and the noise and the food smells.

"You want some cotton candy?" Cielle walked toward the food area, but then saw Darren, and made a sharp left behind the cotton candy stand.

"Oh, no," Helen said, and grabbed her elbow and turned her around. "You're not going to hide."

"He's with Janice Beams!" Cielle felt like the air was pushed out of her lungs.

"You go up to him right now and ask why he didn't show at our house."

"Let's go home."

"If you don't, I will."

Helen pushed Cielle out from the side of the stand, and Darren and Janice were right there.

"What a surprise," Helen said. "We just came from your house, Darren."

"My house?" he asked.

Janice wore a kelly-green dress and kelly-green ribbon tied in a bow around the top of her ponytail. She was a year ahead of Cielle and was the kind of girl who wore a pearl necklace, sat so straight she had to have had a board tied to her back, and clicked her fingernails on the tabletop while people spoke.

"You were supposed to pick up Cielle at five p.m."

Janice tilted her head to the side and looked at Darren with a tight, fake smile.

"I'm sorry," Darren said, but Cielle wasn't sure to whom he was apologizing.

"We drank whiskey at your parents' house," Cielle said.

"You shouldn't have gone to my house," he said.

"Well, we did," Helen said.

"You two are strange," Janice said, shaking her head and strumming her fingers on her arm.

"You don't know us from Adam," Helen said.

"I know your father's dead. I know you date Bodie Mitchell. I know you're strange," Janice said.

"You're not invited into this conversation," Cielle said.

The cotton candy lady handed the swirled pink nest of spun sugar to Janice, who plucked off a piece and stuck it in her mouth.

"I also heard you might lose your farm," Janice said.

Cielle shook her head and stepped close to Janice. Janice leaned back, so Cielle leaned in closer and grabbed her upper arm and squeezed. "Janice," she said. "Janice, shut up."

Janice took another step back and shook her arm. "Fine," she said. "Don't touch me."

Cielle let go and turned back to Darren. "Why did you lie about your brother?" she asked.

He uncrossed his arms.

"Your mother was drunk. She took out Christian's violin and asked me to play," Cielle said.

"His mother's always drunk," Janice said.

"Shut up, Janice," Darren said.

Janice's nose twitched and she stopped eating. The cotton candy lady leaned out of her stall to listen.

"My brother may as well be dead."

"But he's not," Cielle said.

"He's not the same."

"But he's not dead."

"He's in a veterans' home in Washington, no leg, doesn't know his name, he chain-smokes, and a nurse named Lena gives him baths," Darren said. "He's as close to god-damn dead as you get."

"Darren." Janice swatted his shoulder. "Don't cuss."

"Goddamn goddamn goddamn." Darren grabbed the cotton candy from her hand and flung it through the air. It landed on the roof of the stand and looked like a pink bird roosting.

Janice had hate in her eyes, stomped her foot, and turned and walked away. "I'll be in the car," she yelled. "You're all rude and crazy. Don't make me wait." Cielle watched Janice's ponytail and green bow disappear into the crowds and noise.

"I'm sorry," Darren said. "Janice lives next door and came over demanding I bring her tonight."

The cotton candy lady held out a new stick of spun sugar toward them. Helen took the cotton candy and they stepped away from the stand.

"I don't like liars," Cielle said to Darren.

"Sometimes people can be dead to you without having died."

"I wouldn't know that."

"Then you're lucky."

"Some luck."

"I didn't mean it that way. I'm not getting anything right. I'm sorry," Darren said. He shrugged his shoulders. "I'm really sorry. I'm going to go." He turned and walked into the crowds and noise.

"That was awful," Cielle said.

Helen held out the cotton candy, so Cielle ripped off a piece and ate it.

"Let's at least go on the Ferris wheel while we're here," Cielle said. She and Helen moved in the direction of the circle of light turning around and around ahead of them.

CHAPTER SEVEN

On Monday afternoon her mother left $400 in an envelope on the kitchen table and a note: *In Richland Center. Please get this to Mr. Skaar.* Cielle tucked the envelope into her skirt pocket and rode her bicycle to the funeral home. She pedaled up hills and her thighs burned. The bicycle chain and frame rattled. She passed the Lund farm, and Erik, who was in her class, and was baling hay on the tractor. He waved and she waved back. She passed the Daly farm, where Hazel, who was not much older than Helen and already a war widow, tended her garden, her red hair poking out from under a straw hat, her baby lying on a blanket nearby. She passed the Westrum barn — it was white and stone and five times the size of their barn — the biggest barn in Richland County. She kept pedaling uphill, toward the Richardson Funeral Home and Mr. Skaar.

She didn't know what the truth meant anymore, what part of it mattered, or what part was right or wrong. People made up their own truths and ways to live with lies, and maybe it had always been like that. One thing she knew was that people needed to have answers to make sense of their lives. She felt the need to know her father after his death — it was an impulsive need, a blaze in her heart. The heart seemed a dangerous thing, especially when full of secrets or unanswered questions.

The more she discovered, the more she found she did not know. Just weeks ago Mr. Bead had told them about Heisenberg's uncertainty principle in physics: when you try to measure a particle, it becomes a blur, elusive. The observer becomes part of what is being observed, which makes the outcome about interpretation. Mr. Bead had asked, "Does this mean that the ultimate truth is unknowable, immeasurable?"

She leaned her bicycle against the steps of the funeral home. *Maybe,* she thought, *the only certain thing in this life is uncertainty.*

It was dark and cool inside the funeral home. The floor creaked under the worn red carpet. At the end of the hallway the door had a plaque on it that read OFFICE. Cielle patted her pocket for the envelope and walked ahead. She wondered how many dead people were in the home at that moment — how many waiting for viewings and goodbyes, waiting to be buried and returned to the earth.

Cielle knocked on the door and Mr. Skaar opened it.

"Miss Jacobson," he said, "you made it." He stepped aside and waved her in.

The office was simply furnished. He had an oak desk in the middle of the room and a lamp with a green glass shade. A Bible was on one corner of the desk and a picture frame was on the other.

"How old are you?" Mr. Skaar asked.

"Almost sixteen."

He turned the picture frame on his desk toward Cielle and pointed to the girl in the photo with white-blond hair and deep blue eyes. "My daughter, Ingrid, is twelve."

"She's pretty," Cielle said.

"Do you know her?"

"No."

He sat in the chair behind his desk and turned the photo back toward himself. "I see death every day but I hate the thought of dying."

Cielle nodded toward the Bible. "But you believe?"

"I try," he said. "But death makes you

question everything, doesn't it?"

Cielle took the envelope out of her pocket and held it up. "I have this."

"I'm sorry," he said. "You caught me in a thinking mood today." Mr. Skaar didn't reach for it or say anything, so she put the envelope on his desk. He looked at it and then dragged it toward himself with his forefinger.

"It should be the right amount."

He kept his finger on the envelope and nodded his head up and down. Cielle stood so still she felt all her weight on the bottom of her feet.

"I knew your father. He was a good man." He shifted in his chair and tightly laced his fingers together on top of the desk. "Is there anything you want to tell me about his death?"

"He's dead," she said. "There's nothing left to tell."

He pursed his lips together and looked to his right as if someone were there to give him direction. He stood and pulled open a cabinet drawer. He shifted files and lifted a yellow one out and laid it on his desk. It was labeled with her father's name, Lee Gustave Jacobson. "What I'm wondering," he said, and put the file on the desk and opened it, "is if this was a suicide made to look like an accident, or something else?"

She felt light-headed and thick, like the day she found her father in the barn. She heard the air pass in and out through her nostrils, and felt her pulse in her eardrums. What could he do? He'd already examined and embalmed the body and let it go into the grave.

"By law, I'm required to report suicide or foul play," he said.

"You reported an accident," she said.

"Out of respect." He tapped the file. "But these photographs tell another story, and it's been eating at me."

She didn't know what he wanted right then: to know the true story for himself, or report something to the police or Old Mr. Olsen. Would it matter what she told him, if she told him anything? Her eyes met his. Outside, crickets trilled. The golden summer sun streamed through the window and glittered on the floor like light coming through water.

"He's dead and you have your money," she said, and there was nothing more to say.

She stopped at Five Points Cemetery on the way home. She walked to her father's grave, where the mound of dirt was fresh, with his body in the ground, and not far away there were mastodon bones in the ground, and other people from other times, and Indian bones and more arrowheads scattered and covered — layers of life in the earth — all of what had come and gone. One day she'd be gone, but she didn't know where she'd be or what ground would claim her.

She lay on her back on the grass next to him. She watched the clouds shape-shift and told him what she saw: a fish, a dragon, a heart, a winged angel. "I'm sorry you were sad and I didn't know it," she said. She reached out and put her hand on the dirt. "Things have gotten messy. Secrets are dangerous, hurtful things." She stayed there a while longer, watching the sky and not saying anything. She shut her eyes and imagined the spin of the earth, and thought of the greatness of the unknown.

That night, Cielle lay in bed wide awake and fully dressed. She watched the shadows from the porch light that projected swaying tree branches on her walls and ceiling. The shadows calmed her. The gray-black branches swayed and slipped. She turned on her side and there was a white moth at her window. Its wings fluttered and glowed along the dark edge of the frame. The moth hovered as though it wanted to come in. Everyone wanted in, she thought, they wanted to be home, to know what they couldn't know and not be afraid in the dark. Then the moth latched on to the screen and sat still with its wings closed. It hung on, with its tiny little legs as thin as strands of hair; it hung on, a little white dot in the dark.

Outside, it was darker than the feathers of a crow. It was close to midnight, and there was no moon, only hazy smudges of starlight behind the cloud layer. Cielle rode her bike back to the funeral home while Boaz slept. A few porch and barn lights shone sturdy and still in the distance, proof of life. She came to a stretch of road surrounded by woods. The air cooled, and in front of her was a tunnel of black, where the definition and shape of the world disappeared, and she felt she was falling into a well, reeling through dark matter, waiting to hit bottom.

She parked her bike behind the building. She took a flashlight from her satchel, clicked it on, and held it under her armpit, then pulled a hairpin from her pocket, bent it straight, and jiggled it in the back door's lock until it opened. She went to Mr. Skaar's office; the door was unlocked and she found and lifted out her father's yellow file from the cabinet. She put it in her satchel and left the way she came in.

CHAPTER EIGHT

The next morning Cielle's grandmother had her up and outside by seven. The tractor rumbled and sputtered. The diesel exhaust caught in the back of her throat.

"Climb up," her grandmother said. She kept her hands on Cielle's lower back as Cielle climbed into the tractor seat. Her grandmother had cut and baled hay before; she'd done it most of her life. The seat vibrated from the rattling motor and tickled Cielle's legs. Her grandmother hoisted herself up and rolled her sleeves to her elbows.

"Shove over. We have to share this seat. Are you too big to sit on my lap?"

"I don't know." Cielle positioned herself on her grandmother's thighs.

"You're tall, but light as a bird. I'll be the feet and shifter. You steer. I could do this in my sleep."

"Which way?"

"Straight. At each end do a full turn to start a new row. We cut first, bale later."

The tractor bumped along; the spinning shears cut the alfalfa grass and left it in place on the ground. The grass smelled bitter and pungent like cut spring onions.

It took close to two hours to cut half the field. Cielle and her grandmother were hot and sweating. Her grandmother leaned in close to her ear and said, "Time for a water break, do one last row."

Cielle nodded and stood to make the last turn in time. Her pants were damp and clinging to her thighs, her butt, and her waist. The tractor jolted over a bump, and Cielle pitched forward. She struggled to regain her stance and held on to the wide, round steering wheel for balance while her grandmother grabbed her at the waist. Out of instinct, Cielle patted her pants pocket but it was turned inside out. Air escaped her lungs. She turned as the folded note tumbled behind the tractor, into the shears.

Her grandmother braked and turned off the engine.

"What was it?" her grandmother asked.

"Move." Cielle jumped down to the ground and onto her hands and knees behind the shears. She picked through the grass for the pieces of paper. Tears fell from her eyes. The ground blurred in greens and browns and specks of white.

"What was it?" A strand of white hair was matted against her grandmother's forehead like a streak of paint.

"I'll find it all," Cielle said.

"It's gone."

"It's here." Cielle pulled as many pieces of paper as she could from the shears. The grass and dirt were warm from the heat. She stuffed torn paper into her pockets. Some pieces were blank or had a word or two. Some were smeared with black grease and green grass stains.

She'd been carrying the note as if her father were always just about to tell her something. As if his last words hadn't yet been spoken. As if he were far away and sending news from a different part of the world.

Her grandmother lowered onto her hands and knees next to Cielle. "Is that what I think it is?"

"This was my fault," Cielle said.

"No, it wasn't. Why didn't you tell me?"

"How could I?"

Out of the corner of her eye, Cielle saw movement. Her mother ran out from the house toward them.

"Shit," Cielle said. She'd never seen her

run so fast before.

"Oh, hell." Her grandmother stood with her arms out, hands up. "We're okay, Olive, slow down."

"I told you it was too dangerous," Cielle's mother yelled, out of breath.

"We just dropped something," her grandmother said. "We're okay here."

"Stand up, Cielle," her mother said. Cielle stood. She looked Cielle up and down and grabbed her wrists. "Open your hands."

Cielle held them tightly shut. Her mother squeezed harder and dug her nails in a little. "I need to count fingers!" She pried Cielle's hands open, and bits of paper fell to the ground. Her mother bent over and held ripped pieces of paper. One scrap had two words on it in blue ink. Her eyebrows raised and Cielle knew she recognized the curve of the letters. "You had this?" She turned the paper over and held it up in front of Cielle. *Forgive me,* was written. "Do you know what this letter said?" she asked.

The sun was like a piece of burning metal in the sky. Salty sweat stung at the corners of Cielle's eyes and everything was too bright to look at: the pieces of paper in her mother's hands were blindingly white.

"Well?" her grandmother asked.

Cielle set her jaw and bit on the tip of her

tongue. She shifted her eyes from the house in the distance back to her mother. "I was saving it."

"For what?" her grandmother asked.

"I don't know," Cielle said. "For when I was ready."

"It was just a piece of paper," her mother said. "It was just paper and ink."

Her grandmother bent down to pick up the pieces that had fallen. "The last thing my son wrote was not just paper and ink." She spat on the ground. "And I don't know what you did to make it look like he had an accident, but you have some explaining to do."

"Do you want people knowing your son committed suicide?" Cielle's mother said. "Do you want people calling him chicken-shit or crazy, or for your granddaughters to feel shamed in this town for having a father who chose death over them?"

"I don't want any such thing. I just want the truth."

"Suicides get no funeral, they get no sympathy. Covering this up is self-preservation. About a future for my daughters."

"I'll be in the house," her grandmother said. "When you're ready to sit down and talk, I'll be ready to listen. I'm his mother and I deserve to know. So do his daughters."

Trucks were getting ready to take away the last of the lumber and beams from the barn. Her mother handed the scraps of paper back to Cielle. "I'm sorry. I'm so sorry you had to know this."

"I already knew. I found him in the barn. You don't remember?"

"I don't remember."

"I've known all along."

"I wish you hadn't seen that. No one should see that."

"Too late," Cielle said, and put the pieces of paper in her pocket. "I saw it."

A woodpecker knocked on a hollow tree nearby.

"Foolish birds," her mother said, "banging their heads on trees. Is that tractor's parking brake even on?"

Her mother checked that the tractor wasn't going to move on its own. "Someone will have to put a tarp over this thing since our barn is gone, and what's a farm without a barn? Not that we'll get any more rain this month." She walked toward the men at the trucks.

"How do you know?"

"The almanac says so, and I can feel it. The last ten years were good; we were due a dry spell and that tornado. It's nature's way."

"It wasn't just paper and ink," Cielle said.

Her mother stopped but didn't turn around. "You want to talk about the note?" Her hands were on her hips and each elbow made a perfect triangle of open space.

Cielle did, and she waited.

"Come on." Her mother reached her arm back toward Cielle, but didn't turn to look at her. "Let's go have a talk after we deal with these men."

Workmen stood about the driveway smoking cigarettes, and one stepped out toward them as they came up from the field.

"Everybody okay?" he asked.

"We're fine," her mother said.

"We have some items for you here." He pointed at a canvas tarp. He crushed his cigarette on the bottom of his boot and put the cigarette butt in his pants pocket. He lifted the tarp and kept his eyes on the objects below. There was a wide-brimmed leather hat, a pair of canvas work gloves, black suspenders, a coil of rope, and a wooden beam with engravings on it that read, *Helen loves Bodie,* and, below it, *Lee loves Olive.* Her father's engraving looked fresh, the letters light-colored and soft where the knife had carved into the wood-flesh.

"I thought . . ." the man said.

"Yes, thank you." Her mother reached down and picked up the rope. "But get rid of this."

He handed it to one of his men and they threw it in the truck as if it were a hot potato. "We made a pile of good wood under the oilcloth tarp, if you want to keep any of it for rebuilding."

"We won't be rebuilding."

He lit another cigarette. "We're done, then."

"You're done."

"Storm did most of the work." He picked at his teeth for loose tobacco with a dirty fingernail. "Except for the foundation, hay, and bird shit, it's like a barn was never here."

"Watch your language when you're speaking to women." Her mother pulled the tarp back over the objects.

"Excuse me, ma'am."

Cielle looked at where the barn had been just over two weeks ago. The foundation was like an open wound — bare, exposed, un-protected.

"Any fool would know a barn had been here," Cielle said. "A good barn. This is a farm and there's a giant foundation and a hole in the ground."

The men snickered and kicked at the dirt.

He raised his hand to shake her mother's but she didn't move, so he tipped his hat and turned on his heel. "Good afternoon, Mrs. Jacobson." The men climbed into the truck, the engine coughed to life, and they drove away.

Cielle sat at the kitchen table while her mother was on the phone.

"Yes, Mrs. Olsen," her mother said. "I'll talk to the girls and we'll get back to you." She hung up.

"What did she want?" Cielle asked.

"To help."

"She's a drunk."

"Cielle."

"I've seen it."

"Don't you spread that rumor."

"Just saying what I've seen."

"She thanked us for returning their mailbox and offered her professional services for free. She said she'd come talk and help you through your emotions."

"She doesn't want to talk to us."

"No, she wants you to talk to her."

"No, thanks."

Her mother took utensils out from drawers. "That's fine. I don't blame you. I wouldn't want to talk to a stranger either. I have to make a cake for your sister's birthday tonight. Get the flour and sugar down for me. She wants a white cake with coconut frosting. I've been stocking up the rationed butter and sugar for months."

"Where's Helen?"

"I don't know where your sister goes half the time."

"Besides, can't we just talk to you about how we feel?"

"What is it you want to say?"

There was a creak on the stairs. Her grandmother stepped down from the bottom step and crossed her arms. She'd bathed and her hair was wet, and her face was still flush from the heat and sun.

"She wants to know about the note, Olive. She wants to know what had been going on, and how you feel about all this. I want to know too."

"The note gave nothing. No reason, no excuse," her mother said.

"Then what did it say?" her grandmother asked.

"It said, *I'm sorry;* it said, *I love you.*"

"Does Helen know anything?" Cielle asked.

"I don't think so." Her mother reached

for the heavy bowls on top of the icebox. Cielle noticed her father's mug was gone.

"Where's the mug?" Cielle asked. "I said not to touch the mug."

"I washed it out, Cielle. It had old coffee in there." Her mother placed two clay bowls side by side on the wooden island. "And besides, I didn't want to look at it every day."

Cielle turned to look for the boots by the door. They were still there, dusty and crumpled side by side. "Do not remove those." She pointed at the boots. "Do you hear me?"

"You're very loud." Her mother opened a drawer and took out a whisk and measuring cups.

"Do you understand?" Cielle asked.

Her mother busied herself measuring ingredients and ignored her.

It was the small things that stuck in Cielle's mind. The photos lined up on the porch held down by stones. The coffee mug. The boots. Objects in and out of the house as if he'd return the next day or the day after that. These were the artifacts he left behind, proof of his life, things she could use to piece together the meaning of his time on earth. It had been the unread note — words not yet spoken, words waiting —

that made her feel as if he could be alive somewhere, somehow. Paper and ink gave the dead a voice. The note wasn't enough and never would have been enough. She knew that. But it had been something, and now it was gone.

"Mother?" Cielle asked. "Do you hear me?"

"Quit this nonsense," her mother said.

"He had to have said something more in the note," her grandmother said.

"He said, *My head is a throbbing ache as I write this, my nerves worn out. I am a beaten man.*"

"He said that?" Cielle asked.

"He was sick, Cielle. He didn't let you see it, but he carried a darkness inside. He felt heavy and lost. Life was hard and complicated for him. He'd been that way his whole life."

"Why didn't he go to the doctor for medicine?"

"There isn't any medicine for sadness."

"It's true," her grandmother said. "Lee always had a nervousness and sadness about him."

Her mother cracked another egg into the bowl and whisked the eggs. She measured the sugar and stirred it in hard and fast.

"What's done is done," her mother said.

"That's what I think. That's how I feel. For some things there is no reason, no explanation or answer, and you have to move forward. Life goes on." She poured the flour into the bowl all at once and a small cloud of dust rose, and she shut her eyes.

"I don't know if I can accept that," Cielle said.

Her grandmother sat in a chair at the kitchen table. "Resisting what is will keep you stuck in hurt," she said.

"I'm not resisting. I'm confused, I'm sad."

"We all are," her mother said.

"You don't just move on," Cielle said.

"It's all you can do," her mother said.

"It's only been sixteen days." Cielle stomped her foot on the floor. "Sixteen! Days!"

"Okay." Her mother stopped her mixing and looked at her. "I know."

"God," Cielle said, her face hot and her eyes tearing. "Goddammit!" She went upstairs, put on her riding pants and boots, and came back down. "I'm going for a ride at the Mitchells'," she said, and left.

It was still early morning. She brushed Ginger in her stall, down her neck and legs, then down from the top of her back. Dust and hay flew into the air and she brushed her harder to make the coat shine. "I bet that feels good, girl. It's been a while." She scratched Ginger between her ears and Ginger bowed to her touch.

She heard footsteps and Mrs. Mitchell entered the barn.

"Trail ride?" Mrs. Mitchell asked.

"If that's all right."

"Mind if I come along?"

"They're your horses," Cielle said.

"All right, then." Mrs. Mitchell brushed and readied Juno, the bay mare, to ride. She had a smile on her face.

"Something to be happy about?" Cielle asked.

"Just glad to be going for a ride."

Cielle hefted the saddle onto Ginger's back and tightened the girth around her belly. Ginger stomped, snorted, and nodded her head up and down.

"She hasn't been ridden since you last saw her," Mrs. Mitchell said.

"You should have exercised her."

"She wouldn't let me on her."

"She always lets you ride her."

"I think she was waiting for you."

Cielle knew Mrs. Mitchell was watching her, and she wasn't in the mood. She just wanted to take a ride and clear her head. She led Ginger out of the stall, adjusted her hard hat, and swung herself up into the saddle.

"I'm going to start on," Cielle said, and clucked her tongue. Ginger walked forward, out into the sun. She steered Ginger to the field behind the barn, along the tree line and toward the cherry orchard. There were trails throughout the woods and if the sun got hot enough she'd take them for shade, but it was still early, not yet ten in the morning, and large white clouds hung in the sky. The sun was warm and there was a breeze, and it felt good on Cielle's skin. She took a deep breath: leather, horse, grass, honeysuckle. The clank of hooves, the sway of the animal, and the sway of her own hips calmed her. If this was moving on, then she would get on this horse every day and move in a direction that felt like forward. The sky was bright blue, the trees were full and green, and orange tiger lilies in bloom lined the side of the pasture.

Ginger sidestepped and whinnied. She wasn't one to spook or act out. The pounding roll of Juno cantering came closer. Cielle sat up straight and deeper in the saddle, tightened her legs, and pushed her heels down in the stirrups.

"Okay, okay, Ginger. We're good." She tried to get Ginger to sit still, but the horse backed up. Cielle pressed hard into Ginger's belly with her heels and clucked her tongue but Ginger wouldn't move forward. Mrs. Mitchell slowed Juno to a trot and then to a halt right up next to Cielle and Ginger.

"She's been funny," Mrs. Mitchell said. "Give her a swat on the butt."

"What happened?"

"Nothing." She lifted her leg to adjust her stirrup. "Animals sense things. They feel our energy and react to it."

"I don't like to hit her."

"If she senses you're in control, she'll be more comfortable. If she feels you're anxious, then she gets tense and jumpy."

"I'm not anxious."

"Well, whatever it is."

"I'm nothing."

"You're different than you were before." She dropped the stirrup and settled her foot on it.

"I'm still me," Cielle said.

"Sweetheart." Mrs. Mitchell dropped her reins and Juno lowered her head and stood perfectly still like she might take a nap. Mrs. Mitchell unbuttoned the cuffs on her shirt and rolled up her sleeves. "You'll never be the same."

Cielle didn't want to believe she'd changed so much in a matter of sixteen days that even a horse could tell. This was the first time she'd ever been aware that she was in a process of change, and could decide who she'd become, or at least try as hard as she could to be a certain way. She had no idea what kind of woman she wanted to be.

"She'll follow Juno. Where do you want to go?"

"Cherry orchard."

They walked through the open pasture, and Ginger relaxed and closely followed Juno. The grass was tall, and ahead of them it shifted like waves from the wind — it leaned, rose up, leaned again, undulating in light greens drying out into yellows. The tick-ticking of the grasshoppers and cicadas beat out, that heated sound, that ticking of gas stoves, of fire.

Mrs. Mitchell's hair was a short bob cut — honey-brown, straight and fine, and held back from her face with clips on either side. She was athletic and sturdy, comfortable on a horse, a good rider, and Cielle felt lucky to have learned about horses from her. If she weren't a woman, she would have been widely respected for her horsemanship.

Cielle wondered what things she herself wouldn't get to do or say because she was a woman, and wondered about the choices

her own sister was making. Helen was willing to wait for a man to let her know when
he was ready to be with her, let her know
when he was ready to have her in his life.
She knew Helen was afraid that if she left
Boaz, Bodie wouldn't be hers anymore; she
wanted to be married young and have a
husband above all else. Cielle wasn't willing
to give up everything that mattered to her
for that — not her independence, her
opinions, or her dreams. That didn't seem
like love to her, to give herself up to wait
for or follow someone else.

Mrs. Mitchell turned her head to the side
and said, "Want to talk?"

"Did my mother call to say I was coming?"

"No."

"I know it was suicide. I knew that day."

Mrs. Mitchell stopped and Ginger almost
ran straight into Juno's behind. She turned
Juno fully around, and walked her up until
her foot touched Cielle's and their knees
and toes met, as if they were pieces to a
puzzle linking together. The horses didn't
mind the proximity.

"How did you know?"

"I found him."

"Oh, Cielle."

"Do you know why?" Cielle asked.

"His headaches depressed him. He wanted to get better. He tried, Cielle."

"Did he?" Cielle looked over at the trees: Douglas fir, blue spruce, paper birch, elm, oak, locust, maple, and weeping willow. And the wildflowers: tiger lily, honeysuckle, black-eyed Susan, buttercup.

"If anyone knew what his state of mind was like, it might have been Mrs. Olsen. He saw her for counseling. No one else knew he was seeing her. Not even your mother. I saw him coming from their house one day, and he asked I keep it a secret. He was embarrassed he couldn't help himself." She put her hand on Cielle's knee. "But had I known how bad it was, I would have said something."

Cielle nodded.

"I'll tell your mother, but right now she doesn't want to hear any of it."

"I know."

"Are you okay?"

"I don't know. I had this note he left, but it got ruined."

Mrs. Mitchell nodded.

"And then Bodie and this war. It's too much all at once."

"Sometimes not thinking about any of it helps. I want to show you something before we go to the orchard," Mrs. Mitchell said.

"There's a track where the horses love to run. I think we could use a good run." She steered Juno into an adjacent field and trotted through tall grass to a maple tree at the top of the hill, and Cielle followed. At the top of the hill was a dirt racetrack. The minute Ginger was on the track she bolted into a gallop without a cue from Cielle, as if a horse's instinct was to run on an open dirt loop.

Cielle leaned forward, loosened the reins, gripped the horse's mane, squeezed with her thighs, and let Ginger run. She didn't want to stop, ever. "Go, go, go," she whispered. Ginger's legs drummed and pounded beneath her. This was freedom and power. This sunshine and this speed and this air on her face, through her hair, this live gorgeous animal running just to run, this muscle and heart and earth beneath her, was beautiful. Her eyes watered. She'd never felt more alive or happier than in that singular moment. There was a log jump between two maple trees. Ginger soared over it with ease. They flew through the air for seconds that seemed like minutes — airborne, suspended, flying — then Ginger landed and didn't miss a step and galloped around the track again. Cielle smiled, she couldn't help it. Her eyes watered, she leaned down, hung on. Drumming legs, dirt and dust and wind and speed. She thought, *There's nowhere else I'd rather be.*

As Cielle rounded the track she saw Mrs. Mitchell and Juno headed for the log-jump. Cielle came around the bend in time to see Juno push forward off her back legs, her haunches flexed, sweaty, and muscular. She took off too early and lurched to clear the log, and Mrs. Mitchell whipped back in the saddle like a rag doll and then swung forward, too far forward. She lost her stirrups and was up on Juno's neck. Cielle hoped she'd scoot back into the saddle, or get low enough and use her legs to hold on. But the forward momentum was too strong, and Mrs. Mitchell sailed into the air over Juno's head, doing a somersault and landing on her back. Cielle steered Ginger off the track at full gallop toward them. She dug her heels in and Ginger galloped harder and faster than she'd ever galloped before.

Mrs. Mitchell was on her back while Juno stood by a tree eating grass as though nothing had happened. Cielle dismounted, shaky and out of breath, her chest buzzing as though there were a million tiny flies inside. She knelt beside Mrs. Mitchell.

"Are you all right? Can you hear me?"

Mrs. Mitchell's eyes were closed and she

parted her lips but then closed them again.

"I can get you on Juno and lead you back."

Mrs. Mitchell opened her eyes and shook her head back and forth in tiny motions. "I'm too heavy," she said. "I need to lie here a minute and catch my breath."

Cielle reached for her hand, and Mrs. Mitchell gave it a light squeeze. "I'm okay, Cielle. I just bruised my tailbone real bad. Ride back, take Juno with you, and get Bodie or Jim to pick me up in the truck."

A pressure rose up within Cielle, fast and unexpected, and her body took over — she sobbed, heaved, and hiccupped, bent down, head in her hands, and let it come. She felt ashamed but couldn't stop. She was so tired. She caught her breath and yawned, then wiped her eyes so she could see.

"Good," Mrs. Mitchell said. "You needed that."

"I'm sorry."

"I know you're scared and sad." She reached up and took Cielle's hand. "I know."

Cielle nodded. "I'll go get someone to come for you."

She held Juno's reins, and mounted Ginger, who sidestepped again. "Not today, Ginger," Cielle said, swatting her hard on the ass, and Ginger quit it.

"Don't be reckless," Mrs. Mitchell said.

Cielle clucked her tongue. Ginger and Juno picked up a trot and then a canter, running in unison, keeping pace. She hoped Mr. Mitchell and Bodie were home. If not, she'd leave Juno at the house and ride the miles home to get her own mother. The horses pushed forward as if they knew their mission was to help their owner, to save the downed, to heal the wounded. Instead of riding back the way they'd come along the edge of the field, Cielle cut straight across to get to the farm faster. The tall dried grasses swooshed and snapped underneath her, against the horses' hooves and forelocks. The horses ran steadily over the bumpy ground and through the thick grasses.

Don't be reckless, don't be reckless. She couldn't promise that. She had a fire inside her as if someone had dropped a hot coal in her gut. She was not going to be quiet. She was not going to be well mannered, unsuspecting, or go unnoticed. Her mother said for some things there were no answers, but that didn't mean she couldn't look for them. It didn't mean she just walked away, or gave up. Some people didn't want to know things, but Cielle always wanted to know things.

There was movement ahead. A flock of starlings, hundreds of them, lifted from the tops of the trees at the edge of the pasture and rose, a swarm of small black dots moving as a whole against the blue sky like pepper. They swooped down in one motion, almost as if to skim the tips of the grasses, and lifted again, rising, rising, and veered out of sight, off to who knows where. Here and gone.

CHAPTER NINE

Mr. Mitchell rode Juno out to the track to be with Mrs. Mitchell, while Bodie pitchforked hay into the flatbed of the pickup, over which he would lay a blanket where they could put his mother to drive her back. Helen stood and watched.

Cielle pulled a round peppermint candy from her pocket and fed it to Ginger. "So, have you two had any talks lately?" Cielle asked.

"Don't test me, Cielle," Bodie said. "Not while my mother's lying out there."

"What's this about?" Helen asked.

"She's pushing buttons," Bodie said. "Mind your own business, Cielle."

"I think everything should be in the open, is all I'm saying," Cielle said.

"All right." Bodie raised the pitchfork and rammed it into the dirt so it stood on its own. "You want me to tell Helen right now?"

"I'm not going to tell her for you," Cielle said.

"What in hell are you two talking about?" Helen asked.

Bodie spit and then turned toward Helen and crossed his arms tightly over his chest. "I enlisted in the Army Air Corps back in November. I go to Texas in a few weeks for training."

"You are not going," Helen said. "You are not leaving in a few weeks."

"I am," Bodie said.

"And when were you going to tell me, and why did Cielle know this? Why did you know this and not tell me?" She looked at Cielle.

"Because he had to tell you."

"I told Cielle a few days ago. I was afraid to tell you."

"You should have been afraid. What about me?"

He pulled the pitchfork from the dirt and climbed up onto the flatbed. "You know what, Helen, this is bigger than us. This is about going to fight for our country. This is about being a man, and getting out of this middle-of-nowhere heart farmland to do something that matters."

"It's the heartland," Cielle said under her breath, while adjusting Ginger's saddle and

168

tightening her girth.

"It's the what?" Bodie asked. He looked angry enough to stick the pitchfork through her torso.

"Heartland," Helen said. "It's the heartland."

"Whatever," he said.

"The middle, the center, the heart of something," Cielle said.

"Lay off it, Cielle," Bodie said.

"Besides that," Helen said, "I should matter too."

"You do matter."

"But there's something that matters more."

"Don't start."

"We talked about marriage and then you made this decision on your own without taking me into account or asking how I felt, and you expect me to be okay with that?"

"Everyone supports this war, it seems, except for you."

"This isn't about the war, Bodie. It's about us making decisions together."

"I don't know."

"What don't you know?" Helen stood at the edge of the truck, her hands up in the air. "What?"

"You just want so many things." He didn't look at her.

"I want to be married to you. I want to have a family with you. I don't want you to die at war. Is that too much to want?"

"No." His head lowered further, his chin closer to his chest. The pitchfork made an awful scraping sound against the metal of the truck bed as he shuffled the hay around. "But I'm going to Texas, because that's what I want."

Helen shut her eyes and put her hand over her mouth. Cielle saw the deep breaths she took to keep herself together, and wished she'd yell at him, but she didn't. She wished she'd bang on his chest or hug him so tight he'd change his mind, but she didn't.

"I don't expect you to wait for me," Bodie said.

"I can't believe this is coming out of your mouth." Helen shook her head back and forth. "Why have you been wasting my time?"

"Wasting your time?"

"You knew I wanted things you didn't want, but you told me you loved me, that you wanted to marry me. But you don't. You lied and you wasted my time. Time I could have spent moving on and making other plans. You're a coward."

"I'm sorry you see it that way."

"You don't get it."

"I made this decision long before your father died, and when he died I didn't know how to tell you I'd just been called for training."

"You can't even look at my face."

Bodie kept his head down. *Look up,* Cielle thought. *Look up.*

"Cielle, wherever you're going, I'm going with you. Get me out of here."

"Don't take that horse." Bodie snapped his head up.

"Get on first and scoot back," Cielle said, and held the reins while Helen mounted Ginger. "Best to go get your mother," she said to Bodie. "They'll be waiting for you."

Bodie stood in the flatbed of the truck and banged the pitchfork down. "Do not take that horse!"

Cielle thought he'd regret his choice to enlist and leave, instead of taking the exemption to stay and farm, but he wouldn't ever admit it. She didn't understand why he was more afraid to commit to Helen than to a war and places he'd never been and men he'd never met and danger he couldn't yet imagine. She didn't understand why he'd take danger and the unknown over safety and a possible known. Unless it was his only way out, his only way to see the world beyond Boaz.

Helen was in the saddle. Cielle pulled the reins over Ginger's head, swung her leg over Ginger's neck, and settled into the saddle and stirrups. Then Helen slid down and put her arms around Cielle's waist.

"Your mom will be all right, just slow and sore for a bit," Cielle said to Bodie. "You should drive out to get her."

"She'll be all right, but maybe one day she won't," he said.

"Doesn't that seem to be the way things work? Things happen whether we want them to or not," Cielle said.

"Isn't that the truth?" Helen said, and sat very still on the back of the saddle. "The people you most want to stay, leave."

"I don't know what to say." Bodie dropped the pitchfork and jumped down from the flatbed. "What the hell do you want me to say?"

Cielle felt something catch in her throat and nudged Ginger forward, out of Bodie's reach. "You should say you're sorry," Cielle said.

Bodie kicked the dirt, cursed under his breath, and grabbed at the air. He picked up a rock and threw it at the side of the barn. "Just go wherever it is you're going," he said. "And make sure you get Ginger squared away when you bring her back."

Cielle put her hand on Helen's thigh and looked back. "Ready?"

Helen nodded yes. Tears streaked her cheeks, but she firmly set her jaw and looked straight ahead. Her eyes were so blue through her tears, and in the sunlight Cielle thought they looked as blue as the aquamarine stone in their grandmother's wedding ring. Cielle turned in the saddle, picked up the reins, and trotted down the driveway. Her sister's body was warm and heavy against her own, and it was a comfort.

Once they were on the road Cielle slowed Ginger to a walk. Ginger's hooves clicked beneath them. She wondered if Bodie would come for Helen at the house later, or ever again. Cielle didn't know how he could switch his feelings on and off, or push them somewhere so deep he didn't have to face or feel them. She wondered if Bodie was cold and heartless or afraid and incapable, and then wondered what that made her father. Was there something to help her understand why she and her sister and mother were the kind of women men didn't fight for and stand by, but instead were lied to and left? Was it a flaw of her own, of Helen's or her mother's, like something inherited and passed down?

"Is there something wrong with me? Did I

173

do something wrong?" Helen asked, and rested her head on Cielle's back. Cielle felt Helen's chest heave in quiet sobs.

"No," Cielle said. "There's nothing wrong with you."

"But I'm not enough. I'm not good enough."

Cielle didn't know the answer. It seemed being a good person didn't mean anything at all, it didn't mean you got what you wanted or kept people close or that your life would turn out the way you thought and hoped it would.

"You're smart and beautiful and kind, Helen."

"This isn't the way things are supposed to happen."

"They're happening. Things are happening and we have to deal with them."

"Maybe I shouldn't have left back there. Maybe I should have said I'd wait, no matter what. It's not that I don't support the war. I just don't want Bodie in it."

"Bodie's leaving you, even though he doesn't see it that way. He's leaving you."

"Maybe he'll come back, and I should wait."

"He's already gone."

"It's the war, Cielle. He has to go, and I know that, I just don't want him to."

"He's making decisions without you. If you stay with him you'll be waiting on him your whole life."

Helen was quiet and Cielle knew she understood that, and knew it to be true.

"Maybe it would be better than being alone," Helen said.

"I doubt that."

"I'm scared to be alone."

"You're not alone."

"Dad's dead. Bodie's leaving."

"Men don't make your worth or world, Helen."

"Listen to you," she said.

Cielle didn't say anything. She hoped for someone to love her for who she was and who wanted what she wanted, and she'd wait for it.

"I'm sorry," Helen said.

"What do I know?" Cielle said.

They rode on, east. Honeysuckle bushes grew along the side of the road, and Helen leaned over and plucked the delicate trumpets. She handed one to Cielle and they sucked the sweet juice out of the flowers.

"Where are we going?" Helen asked.

"Olsens' house."

"Do I want to know why?"

"She gave Dad psychotherapy."

"Does Mom know this?" Helen put another honeysuckle flower to her lips.

"No."

"Are you sure you want to say anything at all to Mrs. Olsen? Do we want to go there?"

"We're going there now. We're almost there."

The late morning heated up. It was close to noon. Trees gave shade along the road, until the sisters reached the top of the hill, where the land opened into fields of corn and soybeans, and they were exposed to the bright burning of the sun.

"Is that what you know that I don't know?" Helen asked.

"Dad killed himself. There was no accident."

"No."

"I found him, hanging."

"It's not true." Helen was crying again.

"It is."

"Why?" She felt Helen's tears and heat and heartbeat on her back.

"Who knows?" Cielle said. "His headaches? He was depressed?"

They rode fifteen more minutes, then cut through a field and came up on the Olsens' house from behind. Cielle heard talking and laughing before she saw anyone. It sounded like a celebration. At the front of the house a group of people stood close together. An

American flag hung in its stand next to the front door, and a handmade paper sign read WELCOME HOME!

"Turn around," Helen said.

It was too late. Mrs. Olsen waved them over.

"Hard to hide on a horse," Cielle said, and they dismounted and walked with Ginger toward the house.

"Quite an entrance," Mrs. Olsen said. "You two pretty girls on a horse. It's a happy day. We brought Christian home. Our son is home from the war!"

Helen grabbed Cielle's hand and squeezed it tightly. Mrs. Olsen walked ahead, motioning them to follow. The group parted and Christian was in the middle. He sat in a wheelchair and wore his Army uniform. His left leg was gone below the knee, his hair was combed neatly to one side, parted straight and sharp, and he smiled crookedly.

"Welcome home," Cielle said. She looked him right in the eyes, but he didn't seem to see her. His smile stayed crooked, and spittle formed at the corner of his mouth.

"He can't talk," Darren said.

Mrs. Olsen walked up behind Christian and smoothed down his perfect hair and wiped the corner of his mouth with a handkerchief. "He can understand you, though." She bent down to look at him. "Right sweetheart?"

"He can't walk or talk and probably has no idea where he is or who we are," Darren said.

Everyone hushed.

"Stop it," Mrs. Olsen said. "He's alive."

"Barely," Darren said.

Mrs. Olsen leaned down and kissed Christian's forehead. "Don't you listen to him," she said. "That's nonsense." She wheeled him toward the house and Mr. Olsen caught up with her. They lifted his wheelchair up the steps and into the house and then Mrs. Olsen came back to the door. "We have fried chicken, cold beer, and cake inside to celebrate. Please come join us." She smiled big and kept smiling with all her teeth. Everyone shuffled inside except for Cielle, Helen, and Darren.

"She's going to crack," Darren said. "Once everyone leaves she'll get blottoed."

"Why'd he come home?" Cielle asked.

"They wanted to prove he wasn't dead."

Ginger bowed down and rubbed her face on her foreleg.

"You can tie Ginger to the railing," Darren said. "Stay for cake?"

"I can't," Helen said. "I'm sorry."

"Bodie enlisted," Cielle said to Darren.

"Have him come down for a visit. That'll change his mind."

"I don't think so." Helen took a deep breath and puffed out her cheeks as she exhaled. "I need to go home. I don't want to walk alone. Darren, could you walk me home?"

"Sure," he said.

"Sorry, Cielle. This is too much in one day," Helen said.

"I know," Cielle said.

"I just want to go home." She teared up, bit her cheek, and looked up at the sky.

"We have your birthday dinner tonight," Cielle said.

"Some birthday."

Helen and Darren left, and Cielle looked back at the Olsens' house. The front door was open. She tied Ginger to the railing and walked inside. People stood and sat in the living room, eating fried chicken and chocolate cake and drinking coffee and cold beer. Christian sat in his wheelchair, his back to her, and the end of a violin bow poked out from the crook of his arm. Mrs. Olsen walked over with a plate of cake and handed it to her.

"Thanks," Cielle said.

"He loved the violin so much, I'm waiting to see if he remembers it," Mrs. Olsen said.

Cielle walked closer to Christian. The violin rested in his lap and it looked as if he didn't know what it was or what to do with it. The bow rested on his arm where Mrs. Olsen had placed it, but he didn't hold it or touch it. Cielle squatted in front of him so they were at eye level, but he wouldn't look at her, and his eyes shifted from her forehead to her ear to her neck. She set her plate down on the floor and lifted the neck of the violin from his arm. Suddenly he grabbed it with his other hand and she flinched and let go. His reflex was quick and sharp and he looked her in the eye. The top right corner of his lip twitched.

"Okay," Cielle said. "I was just trying to help. I play the violin too." She was reaching for her plate on the floor when his right foot came off the wheelchair footrest and smashed down on the cake. He continued to look at her.

"Well," Cielle said.

"Oh, dear," Mrs. Olsen said. "The doctor said he'd have muscle spasms he can't control."

"Those muscle spasms have good timing," Cielle said.

Mrs. Olsen lifted Christian's foot, wiped it off with a towel, and took the ruined cake and plate to the kitchen.

Cielle leaned in, close to his face. She blew in his ear and he shifted his head away, but didn't turn to look at her. "What is it with people, Christian?" she asked. "What makes them want to lie and hide and hurt those who love them most?" She stood and moved to walk away, but her heart raced and she felt a pulse in her neck. She leaned in again, this time closer, but then Mrs. Olsen came back from the kitchen, wiping her hands on the towel.

"You telling secrets?" she asked.

"Too many of those going around." Cielle straightened up. "I was telling him how the truth can set you free and help you heal. Don't you think?"

"Some of the time," she said.

"I was hoping you and I could talk about it."

"About healing?"

"About the truth about my father."

Mrs. Olsen cocked her head to the side, put the dish towel on the handle of the wheelchair, and said, "Let's go outside." They walked onto the porch. Mrs. Olsen shut the front door behind them, and turned toward Cielle. She was not smiling. She crossed her arms tightly over her chest and her nails looked like shiny red blades. "I'm not sure what we have to talk about."

The warm breeze fluttered and rattled the paper sign. The American flag whipped like a sail.

"My mother said you called offering your services as a counselor."

"I did."

"You also offered your services to my father."

Mrs. Olsen looked straight out down the driveway, toward the gray road, the drying fields beyond, and to the blue-sky horizon and the nothingness beyond that.

"A lot of people talk to me," she said. "But it's private."

"Then I expect what I'm about to ask you be kept private."

Mrs. Olsen waited.

"I want to know why my father killed himself."

Mrs. Olsen took in a quick breath.

"I want to know what you know and what he told you and why this happened."

Mrs. Olsen's eyes watered and Cielle wasn't sure if it was sadness or her leaky eyes again, or both.

"I found him," Cielle said. "He hanged himself in our barn."

Mrs. Olsen stepped back. She shifted her eyes around the porch as if she were looking for something she'd lost. She covered her mouth and gagged. Then she bent over the railing and threw up.

"Are you okay?" Cielle asked.

Mrs. Olsen held the porch railing tightly and wiped her mouth on the back of her hand. "I'm fine."

"You need to tell me what he talked about," Cielle said.

Mrs. Olsen stood, turned toward the house, and Cielle grabbed her wrist. "Please. Why did he do this?"

Mrs. Olsen shook herself free from Cielle. "I didn't know he did this. I didn't know he would do this."

"How did you not know?"

"How could I know? How does anyone know anything about another person? How did you or anyone else not know?" She breathed in a deep breath. "I need to be inside." She turned, went into the house, and shut the door.

Cielle heard the muffled voices from inside, the whip of the flag, the rattle of the WELCOME HOME! sign, and the wind in her ear, like a small tunnel of white noise. Like the sound of nothing.

CHAPTER TEN

Cielle returned Ginger to the Mitchells' and then walked home. The ground radiated heat. Dry grasses on the shoulder of the road crunched under her feet, and she became heated as she walked. She thought a dry piece of grass might be stuck in the back of her throat. The sun made the top of her hair almost too hot to touch.

She understood why people left a place to start over. She loved Boaz, it was all she knew, but she could imagine the relief of being somewhere without memories or a history. What secrets did people hold so close that they wouldn't talk about them? What did they think they were protecting themselves from? The dead were dead and buried.

The road was a straightaway toward home. In winter she could see the outline of her house from this distance, but now the trees were full and the cornstalks had grown tall enough that she only saw the road ahead, the sky above, and the drying corn standing like soldiers on either side of the road.

Just last winter, in February, when the trees were naked and leggy and the earth frozen into clumps under heavy snow, she and her father walked this same road from the Mitchells' back to their house. Their truck's battery had died and they couldn't get a new one until morning.

"Let's hoof it," her father had said.

"Mrs. Mitchell said she'd drive us," Cielle said.

"Let's get some fresh air. Have a walk together." He lightly punched her upper arm.

Cielle rolled her eyes. "Okay, okay."

They bundled up in their coats, hats, scarves, and gloves and set out for home. It was four o'clock and the sky darkened early into nighttime. The horizon was purple and deep pink, and bled upward into a dark blue and black above them. The tree branches were spindly sculptures, beautifully still against the twilight.

"See there?" Her father pointed to the right of the road, across the cut stubble of the Mitchells' cornfield, his breath little puffs of steam lifting into the air. "That light out there?"

Cielle scanned the distance. There were hills, ridges, and valleys in Boaz and surrounding the town. Not all of Wisconsin was flat as the eye could see. Her father had told her that the southwest region of Wisconsin went unglaciated in the last glacial period, twelve thousand years ago, and because there'd been no glacial drift, it was called the Driftless Area. There were cold-water springs, steep limestone hills, valleys, and meadows. The land had been rooted and solid, yet Cielle thought of things drifting — a twig down a river, a cloud, a leaf falling from a tree, snow blowing across a field, her own body drifting across the lake.

Her father stopped, and so did she. He stepped behind her and pointed over her shoulder. "Focus where my finger points," he said. Then she saw the light, small, like a flashlight. It twinkled between tree branches.

"That's our house," he said. "Do you see it?"

"I see it," she said.

"So now you know where we are and how to get home."

"What if the light's not on?"

"The light's always on."

"Not in the daytime, and sometimes it burns out."

"Find a landmark near the light. That giant oak tree."

"The porch light or the oak tree," she said.

"That's the barn light," he said. "You can tell because it's higher up."

They walked and she kept her eye on the light as if it were the North Star. It was cold and their breath fogged in the air and the light of day was gone.

"It's dark," she said.

"You can still see," he said.

"Barely."

"The longer you're in the dark, the more you'll adjust and the better you'll see."

She couldn't remember the last time she had walked outside at night. The stars filled the sky like confetti. The Big Dipper, Orion's belt, the Pleiades, the Milky Way, and so many other bodies of light and mystery above them. She remembered thinking, *Is there life out there? Is there life after this life?*

"Dad?" she asked.

"Cielle?"

"You ever get afraid?"

"Not really."

"Afraid about what you don't know?"

"If I don't know, then there's nothing to worry over."

"What if something I want to happen

doesn't happen?"

"Then something else will happen."

Their boots scuffled over the dirt, snow, and ice. It felt easier to ask these questions in the dark, while moving. She thought a lot about what she didn't know, and worried about what might happen or not happen.

"What if I don't get into college, or no one thinks I'm any good at anything? What if no one wants me?"

"Then that's their loss and you figure out other ways to get what you want. It doesn't mean you give up. You're too young to worry about these things."

"I'm not too young."

He pulled her in by her shoulder, and she tucked in under his arm as they walked. "So much will happen in your life you can't even imagine. We have little control over most of what happens."

"Then what's the point, if I don't get what I want?"

"You'll end up where you're supposed to be. Sometimes what you want isn't what you need."

"That doesn't seem fair."

"No such thing as fair."

Through the summer thickness, Cielle looked for the oak tree and barely saw the top of it. The barn was gone. Its light was gone forever. And her father was right — things would happen she couldn't even imagine. She was warm and tired from worrying and from being afraid. She wanted to stop thinking so much and just be. All the thinking, all of her what-if's, seemed to lead to sorrow and more heartache and uncertainty.

Darren was still at their house, and Trudy had come over for Helen's birthday dinner. They all squeezed around the kitchen table and ate pork chops, and roasted potatoes, and carrots. It almost felt like a normal night. Her mother didn't question Bodie's absence, and Cielle assumed Mrs. Mitchell had called earlier to explain.

Her mother cut the coconut cake and they took slices on plates to sit in the family room. A small pile of pretty wrapped gifts sat next to the sofa and her mother pointed at the pile with her fork and said, "Let's see what's in those boxes."

Helen opened a present from Trudy first. It was a silver link charm bracelet from Tiffany with her initials engraved on the charm of a heart. It was the fanciest present Helen had ever received, and Trudy was too generous for giving it, even though Cielle knew Trudy's parents had paid for it. Her grandmother gave Helen a hand-knit scarf made from beautiful deep violet wool, to keep her warm in the fall and winter in Madison. Her mother gave her a set of new canvases, paintbrushes, and paints.

There were three gifts left. Cielle handed hers to Helen. It was a box of letterpress stationery with Helen's full name engraved on top — HELEN CAMILLA JACOBSON. And she included a set of stamps. "That's so you keep in touch and write me."

"I'll write. I won't be that far away."

"Far enough," Cielle said.

"Far enough is right," her mother said.

"Leaving home is a necessary part of life," her grandmother said.

"When did it become natural to leave your people and never return?" Trudy asked.

"You've got to learn to live on your own," her grandmother said.

"Who says?" Trudy asked.

"Are you girls planning to stay home and help your mothers cook, clean, and farm instead of taking courses, going to parties, and meeting handsome young men?" Cielle's mother asked.

"We could use you at my house," Darren said. "My mother's no good at housekeeping."

"Nonsense," Cielle's mother said to Darren. "I'm sure she's fine." She put the dirty dishes in the kitchen sink.

No one said a word, and Darren looked down at his plate and ate another bite of cake. "Especially now that my brother's home from the war."

"That's good he's home," Cielle's grandmother said.

"He's not all there," Cielle said and her grandmother nodded in understanding. She thought to say, *He's not all gone either, and Mrs. Olsen knows more than any of us about Dad,* but she kept her mouth shut. She wasn't an expert. She didn't know about wounded soldiers, marriage, being a mother, what makes you drink your sorrow away, or about sadness heavy enough to make you want to end your life.

"What are these other two gifts?" Helen asked.

Her mother wiped her hands on a dish towel and walked back into the room. "One was left in the mailbox this afternoon. The other is from your father."

Helen shuffled over to the gifts. "I'm glad he could make it."

"Your father has had that thing wrapped and in his sock drawer for months," her mother said.

Her grandmother tapped her hand on her

thigh. Cielle wondered if he knew during their winter walk that he would be gone by summer.

"He planned ahead," Helen said.

"I guess so," her mother said.

"Do you know what it is?" Helen shook it near her ear.

"Maybe," her mother said.

"Let's have you open this one first," her grandmother said. She picked it off the floor and handed it to Helen. "It's heavy."

"The mystery present," Helen said.

There was the sound of tires on gravel and Cielle leaned to look out the window. "A surprise someone's here," she said as Matthew's car pulled into the drive.

"If it's Bodie, I'm not interested."

"You have to see him before he goes," Cielle said.

"No, I don't," Helen said.

Her grandmother looked out the window, her eyebrows raised. "It is a handsome young man who's not Bodie."

Trudy looked out. "Handsome indeed."

Helen leaned toward the window. "Relax, everyone, it's Matthew."

"Matthew the lawyer," Cielle said.

"The gorgeous lawyer." Trudy elbowed Helen.

Matthew knocked on the door, and

waited. Cielle's mother's cheeks flushed. "This young man saved Helen's life," she said, as she opened the door and held out her hand to shake his. "She choked on a potato and he saved her at the Bredahl Inn."

He held her mother's hand and looked at Helen. "At your service. Happy birthday."

"Thank you," Helen said. "How did you know?"

"Your mother may have told me and invited me for cake. I hope that's okay." He pointed to the box in Helen's hands. "I see you have my present yet to open. I left it in the mailbox in case I couldn't get off work in time."

Helen tore the light blue paper off the box, then set it on the floor, opened the lid, and lifted out a bulbous potato the size of a football.

He winked at her. "Happy birthday."

"You already said that," Helen said.

"I said it again."

She held up the potato.

"I was thinking a doorstop, a paperweight, in case you get hungry, or just a decoration to remind you of me," Matthew said.

"We owe you a thousand thank-yous for what you did," her mother said.

Helen placed the potato by the kitchen door. "Thanks."

"You didn't know our father, did you?" Cielle asked.

"No," he said. "I'm sorry I didn't."

"He'd marry you to one of these girls if he were here," her grandmother said.

"A man would be lucky to marry any of these girls," Matthew said.

Her mother's smile was so bright, Cielle imagined she was already planning dresses to make, cakes to bake, flowers to grow and arrange, a guest list in alphabetical order, and booties to knit for a grandchild.

"This could be promising," Trudy said. "Be careful what you say."

"I'm always careful with what I say," he said.

"Here, Helen." Cielle's mother extended her hand. "Pick up that little box and come with me." Her mother nodded. Helen picked up the box, took her mother's hand, and was led outside. Cielle, her grandmother, Trudy, Darren, and Matthew followed. Cielle wondered what might be waiting from her father for her sixteenth birthday — another small box buried in his sock drawer? What if there was nothing?

Her mother walked to the shed down the hill behind the house. "Open the box," she said.

Helen lifted the top of box and there was

a key. She pointed the key at the shed. "Grandfather's old car?" she asked.

"Yours," Cielle's mother said. "To come home whenever you want, as often as you want."

Her mother unlatched the shed's double doors, and inside was a pretty, shiny car. It was clean, sturdy, and painted black, with whitewall tires, and burgundy red seats.

"It's a 1935 Plymouth PJ Sedan. When your grandfather passed away and we inherited the car, it was in poor shape and just sat in here for years. Your father fixed it up nicely," her mother said.

"I guess I have to go somewhere now that I have a car. I guess I can't stay in Boaz." Helen twirled the key ring around her finger.

"I'll give you the Wisconsin key chain I won at the fair for your key," Cielle said. "Now you have somewhere to go."

It was late when Cielle walked Darren outside to say goodbye. The sky was cloudless and the stars were bright and spectacular. On clear nights the universe was deeper and fuller than ever. She sensed how small they were in the scheme of things, and hoped she'd remember to look up often and know there was more than where she stood.

"I should get back but I don't want to go,"

Darren said. "All this time I missed my brother, and now I can't stand him."

"Maybe it will get easier," Cielle said.

"It won't get easier, I'll just get used to it."

"I guess that's how things go. I guess that will happen with my father — I'll get used to it."

Darren leaned against the porch. "I wish I could drive away tonight. Go live another life."

Cielle hadn't been many places. She'd been to Madison, Milwaukee, and Chicago, but she'd never seen the ocean. She'd never seen a true mountain. She'd never seen a canyon, a desert, or a jungle. She wanted to see the world. She wanted to know how other people lived. She'd imagined herself on a cobblestone street in London, in a bistro in Paris, on a horse in the plains of Colorado with the spiked peaks of the Rockies in the distance, in a skyscraper in Manhattan. And yet, she couldn't imagine anything but Wisconsin and its soft rolling hills, lush fields, and winding roads, as home.

"Where would you go?" she asked.

"Probably Chicago," he said. "You?"

"The ocean, the mountains, New York City, and Europe."

"You better get busy," he said.

She'd never been on a plane but had had flying dreams. Dreams of twisting and lifting into the sky, straight up or sometimes hovering over the ground through clear air. Through treetops. Through clouds. She'd go up, up, up, and have a view of fields and farms, barns and animals below. A view of Boaz. A view of her life. That flying feeling was exhilarating. It was a feeling of being free, weightless, without boundaries, with the ability to go somewhere, anywhere. It was the feeling of galloping on Ginger around the track. Cielle wanted that feeling always. She wanted to know the world she didn't yet know. Every piece of it. And in that moment, she understood that maybe Bodie did too.

Darren stood up from leaning on the porch. He was close; there was a foot between them. He had an upside-down triangle of freckles under his left eye. She crossed her arms and didn't know where to look, so she looked at the fine definition of his clavicle and the small dip of his neck where a vein pulsed under his skin.

"You have a big life ahead of you." He stepped nearer and put his hands on her crossed arms. He uncrossed them as though untying a knot. She looked at him and a wave of heat swept through her. The back of her neck tingled. She'd never kissed a boy before.

He moved his hands to her waist, to her lower back, and pulled her toward him. She moved forward and kissed him, slowly, softly. She loved the heat of his stomach against hers, of his arms around her, of her hands on his neck and face. In that moment, she understood how easy it could be to open up and love someone. He touched her neck, tucked a strand of hair behind her ear. She felt calm and tingly and warm. She wanted connection: to be understood, chosen, loved, seen, noticed, and known. It felt as though touch could heal her, could make her whole again.

He pulled back, kissed her cheek, found her hands, and held them. "We should do this more often."

"I'd like that."

He leaned in and kissed her cheek again. "Good night, Cielle Jacobson."

"Good night, Darren Olsen."

When he was gone she sat on the lawn and watched the stars. She felt happy and then guilty for feeling happy, but she knew her father would want her to feel happy. She let herself be happy to be alive and to have kissed Darren Olsen. She was glad her father's death had brought Darren into her life. She considered cause and effect, and wondered if that was the law of nature — that for one thing to exist another had to expire, for one thing to happen something else had to happen before it, and always, always, if there was bad, there was good, and vice versa.

CHAPTER ELEVEN

A week passed. She was surprised it took that long for Mr. Skaar to show up at the house. He was in the kitchen with her mother and an older man, and they all sat at the table and drank iced tea.

"Mr. Olsen, this is my youngest, Cielle," her mother said. "And Mr. Skaar, you know Cielle."

"I know Cielle," Mr. Skaar said.

Old Mr. Olsen's heavy eyelids made him look sleepy, but his eyes were blue, bright, and alert. His thick hair was snow-white and mussed-up, and his eyebrows were bone-white bushy things, like little hedges on his face.

"I met you as a wrinkled newborn," Mr. Olsen said, and held his hands apart the length of a loaf of bread. "Now I'm a wrinkled old man." He put his glass on the table, slapped his palm on the table, and pushed back his chair. "And I hear you're friends with my grandson."

"Darren is a friend," she said, and blushed.

"That's nice," he said. "Nice to know I can still make a girl blush. Well, I saw your daddy's obituary in the newspaper, and then Mr. Skaar called to tell me a few other things."

Her mother looked down at her hands. Cielle nodded yes.

"So I came to pay my respects." Mr. Olsen stood. "I knew your daddy and granddaddy. We have history." Mr. Skaar looked ready to talk, but Mr. Olsen held his hand up to cut him off, and then put his hand on Cielle's shoulder and said, "Come outside with me, girl."

He led her out the door to the back of the house and nodded ahead. "Been told you cut that field."

"My grandmother and I cut it," she said.

"You're resourceful."

"We do what we need to do."

"As you should," he said.

She crossed her arms.

"Seems your daddy's death on this farm is a mystery of sorts."

"That's why they called it an accident."

He nodded his head up and down and smiled. "Resourceful."

"Seems we have that in common," she said. "What with all the land you've acquired. You must be a rich man."

"That's fair," he said. "I am. Mostly because I follow the rules. Which here means if a man signs a contract, and that man dies by his own hand, he forgoes his land rights."

"And if he dies in an accident?"

"The family has the option to buy back at the sell price."

"What did my mother say about that?"

"She says it was an accident, and that you found him."

"I did."

"Trouble is, Mr. Skaar said he saw you just over a week ago and showed you a file on your daddy, where there were questionable photographs, but now that file's gone missing." He snapped his fingers. "Poof. Gone. Where do you suppose that file went on its own?"

"I don't recall a file."

"You calling Mr. Skaar a liar?"

"No, sir. I'm saying I don't recall a file."

"You're a smart young lady," he said. He chewed on his lip, and then turned and waved toward the house. Mr. Skaar came out of the doorway where he'd been watching and waiting. He caught up to Old Mr.

Olsen and was talking fast, but Mr. Olsen shook his head no and just held his hand up to silence him.

That night, Cielle couldn't sleep. She had her father's file in her underwear drawer and she wanted it gone. And she couldn't stop thinking about Bodie leaving and if Mrs. Mitchell was okay. Neither Bodie nor his parents had called or come over. Helen wouldn't talk about Bodie, and would go for long walks to who knows where. It didn't make sense to Cielle that Bodie was leaving for training in a place none of them had ever seen, and would ship off even farther away to fight in a war. He could be gone for years. He could be gone forever.

Cielle wanted to see him. She wouldn't be able to live with herself if he got hurt, or worse. The moon grew toward fullness and shone brightly like a lamp on the landscape. Shadow-shapes from trees, power lines, and buildings were black and white in the bright nighttime. It was eleven and she was wide awake. She dressed, took the file, and rode her bike to the Mitchells'. She knew Bodie cleaned tack at night and might still be up in the barn.

She pedaled into the Mitchells' driveway, and leaned her bike against the barn. The house was dark, but there was a light on in the barn. Bodie's figure came to the doorway.

"What are you doing here?" he asked.

"I couldn't sleep," Cielle said. "And I wanted to see you."

"I was planning on saying goodbye."

"Were you?"

"My parents wouldn't let me leave without saying goodbye."

"Would you have come to say goodbye on your own?"

"Sure." He turned back into the light of the barn. Cielle followed. He sat on a stool and picked up his beer and took a swig. "You want one?"

"Yes."

He lifted a bottle from a nearby bucket of cold water, popped off the top, and handed the beer to Cielle. He clinked the neck of his bottle to hers. A strip of leather and a set of knives were on the floor in front of him, and two bridles and oil soap to his right. He picked up a knife and slid it across the leather, back and forth. "I can't sleep either."

"It's almost a full moon."

"It's a lot of things." He stopped, set the knife on his boot, and ran the leather strip over his thigh to dust it off. His hair was getting longer, his curls like coils of gold. Soon he'd have to cut it all off. He put the leather over his knee and lit a cigarette. He seemed older. More serious. Less afraid. As if he had nothing left to lose. How he and she both could change so quickly was something she could not understand. He took a drag off his cigarette and the smoke rose toward the barn light and swirled like a fog above them. She thought about how you never knew what change would come and what it might look like.

"Did your mom make coconut cake for Helen's birthday?" he asked.

"As always."

"Does Helen know you're here?"

"No."

"I'd keep it that way," he said. "Forget about me, Cielle. You and Helen are sisters for life, but once I'm gone I probably won't come back. She'd be mad if she knew you were here."

"You don't get to decide who can and can't care about you. You don't get to choose who loves you. And I think she'd understand why I'm here."

"Go home."

"No."

He shook his head back and forth.

"You love us. We love you. I know that,"

she said.

He ran the knife over the leather strip that rested on his leg. The blade flashed silver in the barn light.

"It's not always enough," Bodie said. He tapped the tip of his forefinger on the blade to test its sharpness.

She finished her drink. "Give me another beer."

Bodie handed her a beer, then a bridle, a rag, and oil soap. "Make yourself useful and clean Ginger's bridle."

She dipped the rag into the bucket of water and oil soap. It smelled rich and woody. She laid the bridle across her lap and ran the rag over each section — the headband, the noseband, the braided reins — and she lifted out the dirt and watched the leather turn dark brown as it soaked up the water and oil. It soaked it up as the land did rain. Boaz and all of Wisconsin needed relief, needed to be washed and cooled and nourished. Too much drought and everything died; not everything could be brought back to life.

"I kissed Darren Olsen."

"First kiss?"

"Yes." Cielle touched her cheek with the back of her hand, and then held the cool beer to her cheek.

"Congratulations."

"Thank you."

"It's nice, isn't it?"

"It is."

They were quiet then for a bit, while they sat in the barn tending to sharpening knives and cleaning tack. She felt her body loosen from the alcohol.

"You have the radio in here?" she asked.

"It's too late for that. It'll wake them up." He nodded toward the house, where his parents slept. "Besides, we should call it a night."

"Bodie, no one will know if you don't go, so don't go," she said.

"I'll know. I could make a difference. I could change something."

"Something will change with or without you."

"I want to see what I'm made of."

"What do you think you're made of?"

"I don't know."

She thought: *I'm blood and tissue, brain and heart. I'm cells, water, night, day, stardust, barn dust, hay, and horse.* She finished cleaning the bridle and hung it on its wall hook to dry, and took the saddle over her thigh to clean. The soft throaty call of a horned owl echoed outside.

"That's nice," Cielle said.

"He's here every night," Bodie said. "Asking who, who, who. I always tell him, I don't know who."

Cielle smiled. "Have you seen him?"

"Never seen him, just hear him. He's always out there, somewhere."

"Like the dead."

"I guess. If you believe in that."

"How long do you suppose people grieve?" Cielle asked.

"However long it takes."

"What if you can't remember what normal felt like in the first place?"

She felt the future wide open and unknown. A person started out with such high hopes, she thought, but never knew, could never know day to day, what might happen. They could be ripped and scattered like a barn after a tornado. And then. Then they had to put themselves back together. The living had to go on living.

"You'll remember it when you feel it," he said.

"I wish I knew what was real and what wasn't."

"This knife is real." He tapped the blade on the cement floor and it clinked. "This barn is real." He stomped his foot on the floor, and loose bits of hay and dust scattered over the cement and rose in the air.

"I mean about how people feel. If you can trust they won't hurt you." Cielle dipped the rag in the oil soap and rubbed it over the saddle seat, and there was the sound of Bodie running the knife's blade over leather: *shush shush, shush shush, shush shush.*

"Sometimes people hurt others on purpose and sometimes by accident, but no matter how good things get, there will always be something that will hurt. Like a little pin that gets stuck in your heart."

"I don't want you to go." She meant it more than she'd meant anything before.

"I know you don't," he said. "And I'm sorry."

Bugs flew into the barn light and whipped around in crazy circles. They moved toward heat and the brightest place. Outside, the rolling call of the great horned owl bounced off the night. She knew Bodie was doing the best he could and what he thought was right. She guessed she was doing the same.

"You still have that burn bin outside?" she asked.

"Back there." He tilted his head toward the back barn door.

She walked to her bike, got the file out from its basket, and walked through the barn and stood in front of Bodie. "Matches?"

He reached in his pocket and held them out. She leaned in to take them and he yanked them back. "First tell me what you're burning."

"Paper."

He lurched fast and grabbed the file from her.

"Give it back," she said.

He opened it, flipped through the photos, and then shut the file. "Jesus," he said. He shut his eyes tightly and ran his hand through his hair. He stood and waved the file in front of him like a fan. "Jesus, Cielle."

She took the file and walked toward the burn bin, and he followed her. They stood in front of it.

"Here," he said, and handed her the matchbox. She lit a match and pulled out a photo at a time, there were five of them, and held the flame to the pointed edge of each one. As the fire melted away the edges of the photos and moved toward the centers, she dropped them, one by one, into the dark heart of the metal bin.

CHAPTER TWELVE

The next morning there were men's voices, the clomping of hooves, the neighing of horses, and the bang and clap of wood outside. Before Cielle even sat up in bed, Helen came into her room.

"What's going on? It's loud," Cielle said.

"Look out the window."

Cielle got up. Close to two hundred men in blue and black clothes, straw hats, and beards carried wood and spread it around the foundation of where their barn used to be. Young girls with braids and boys with bowl cuts tended to the horses and buggies that lined their drive and the road. Women in dark dresses and bonnets carried food into their house. The Amish had come to build them a new barn.

"How did they know?" Cielle asked.

"This is what they do."

"Even for people who aren't like them?"

"We're probably not that different."

The Amish lived down dirt roads without power lines in white clapboard homes that looked like any home, except at night they were dark save for the glow and flicker of candlelight, kerosene lamplight, and fire-light. They kept the modern world at bay — no telephones, no distant voices or songs on radios, no hum of an oven or generator or auto-motor rattle. Instead, Cielle imagined the quiet of their lives, the *poof* of blowing out a flame, the creaking floors and breath-ing bodies, the hiss of wood in a burning stove, cows chewing grass, horses shifting hooves — the sounds of the immediate, known world.

Cielle's mother was on the lawn greeting the women who carried food. They hugged her mother. They wiped their own tears, and followed her mother into the house. Cielle looked in her closet for clothes, and Helen sat on her bed.

"You look tired," Helen said.

Cielle looked in the mirror, and her eyes were puffy, with dark bags underneath. "I couldn't sleep last night."

"I heard you sneak out. Your hair smells like smoke."

Cielle pulled a dress over her head, ad-justed the straps, and slipped on her sandals. "Nothing fits right," she said.

"I can't take all my clothes to Madison, so you can take what I leave behind."

Cielle brushed her hair and tied it into a low ponytail. She didn't want to think about Helen leaving too. She walked to the window. "I can't imagine wearing those clothes, living that life."

"Matthew wants to come visit me in Madison."

"What about Bodie?"

"I love Bodie and I always will. But if he doesn't want me, there's nothing I can do."

She knew love wasn't a weakness, but she didn't think love came and went so fast. She didn't understand how a person could let go of one person and move on to another so quickly. Maybe it was different for her sister and Bodie. Maybe they had more room for love, for different kinds of love. Maybe Cielle was afraid to get hurt, afraid someone else would come along and later tell her he was leaving, or leave without saying anything at all. She knew she wasn't as resilient or quick to recover from that kind of loss.

"I don't know what you think I should do. You know, letting people care about you isn't bad," Helen said.

"I never said it was," Cielle said. "I think you should do what you want to do."

There was a knock on the door and her grandmother peeked in. "Girls, hurry and come down."

"Do they speak English?" Helen said.

"Of course they speak English," her grandmother said.

"Do you know them?" Cielle asked.

"Your mother and I know a few of them. Your father knew most. Get your manners in check," her grandmother said, "and get yourselves downstairs. These good people are building you a barn."

The day was gray, overcast, and humid. The men wore cotton clothes and sweated through their blue and black shirts, smelled like raw onions and mildew, and smiled and nodded as they went about their business. They spoke little except for giving directions. Cielle wanted to know what their lives were like. Was it simpler being at a remove from modern life? Was life more joyful, or was it lonely and scary without an escape, knowing you could only stay in one place, among the same people, for the rest of your life?

Pies and breads and casseroles lined the kitchen counter. The women's bonnets were white linen and the girls' bonnets were black.

One of the men came to the door. It was

the same man from her father's wake.

"Ms. Olive, if I could?" He took off his hat and held it in front of his chest. He waited behind the screen.

"Of course," her mother said. "John, you remember my girls?"

He looked at Cielle and then at Helen and tilted his hat off his chest as if waving to them. "Pleased to see you."

Cielle thought him pleasant-looking. He was clean-shaven and his hair was cut short. She wondered if he was shy or if all Amish men spoke to females with a quiet distance. He shifted his gaze down at the door, and knocked his hat against his chest in small movements.

"Girls, introduce yourselves to these nice women and girls who've brought us their food and prayers." Her mother walked outside to speak with John.

An older girl with hair as blond as corn silk stepped forward and said, "We made sun tea." She handed a mason jar to Cielle. Her eyes had a brightness to them, like sunshine itself.

"Thank you. I'm Cielle, and this is Helen."

"I'm Hannah, and this is Miriam and Sarah."

The girls' eyes went from lamp to lamp, to the telephone and the radio.

"You can fool with anything you like," Cielle said. "You flip the switch or turn the knob."

"And just like that it works?" Hannah asked.

"This is our first time in an English home," Miriam said.

"The wires connect the power lines which feed the electricity," Cielle said.

"Can you see it? The electricity?" Sarah asked.

"It's a current you can't see," Cielle said. "It's dangerous like lightning, so it stays in the wires. You don't want to touch it or it could kill you."

Miriam flipped the wall light switch on and off, on and off. Sarah held the telephone to her ear, then looked at it and hung up. "Someone was there," she said. "Someone's stuck inside that thing."

"No one's stuck anywhere," Cielle said.

"Whoever was stuck inside said your name."

Cielle picked up the phone to listen.

"Hello?" a woman asked.

Cielle said nothing.

"I heard the click, who's there?" the woman asked.

"It's nothing," a man's voice said. "We have the line. Talk."

216

"I heard something," she said. "I don't want people listening. Hold on a minute."

Cielle held her fingers over her lips to shush the room. She covered the mouthpiece with the palm of her hand and pressed the earpiece to her ear. She heard breathing, a cough, and a dog barking. Helen widened her eyes for an answer. Cielle mouthed, *Wait.*

"Anna?" the man said. "Are you still there?"

It was Anna Olsen. Mrs. Olsen.

"He killed himself," she said. "I couldn't save him. I couldn't do anything."

"It had nothing to do with you."

"I didn't see the signs." Cielle heard Mrs. Olsen take a drag and exhale smoke. "But I should have known."

"Sometimes you can't know," the man said. "Sometimes there's no way of knowing."

There was the clink of ice cubes on the other line and she imaged Mrs. Olsen drinking out of a tumbler full of ice and golden liquor, smoking her cigarette, drunk before breakfast.

"Why do you think he did it?" the man asked.

Cielle pressed the phone closer and plugged her other ear with her finger. Her heart pounded in her chest and she shut her eyes.

"Why?" Mrs. Olsen asked.

Why, Cielle thought, *why.* She shifted her weight from one leg to the other. She waited.

"He had bad migraines," she said. "And a melancholy he couldn't explain."

Then Mr. and Mrs. Mitchell and Bodie walked up the drive. Mr. McMahon from the grocery store, Mr. Hammond from the farm down the road, and Darren and Matthew walked up behind them. They carried hammers and tool belts and levels.

"I've seen that melancholy with others. It's something we don't know a lot about."

He was happy, Cielle thought. He was fine.

Helen put her hands on her hips. Cielle held her hand out to stop her from talking, but it was too late.

"Who is it?" Helen asked.

"Shit," Mrs. Olsen said. "Goddammit."

The line went dead.

"Shit," Cielle said. "Helen!" She clicked on the phone for a dial tone and the operator came on.

"Mrs. Jacobson, how may I direct your call?"

"This is Cielle. No call. I thought I heard it ring."

"There haven't been any calls to your house this morning, Miss Cielle."

Helen still stood next to her. "What are you doing?"

Cielle raised her hand again.

"I must be hearing things," Cielle said.

The operator was silent.

"You know how sometimes you think you hear something but you're not sure what?" Cielle asked.

Cielle heard shifting in the background, as if the operator were adjusting papers on a desk.

"I heard my name," Cielle said. "I heard someone say my name."

"I'm sorry for your loss," the operator said.

"Thank you." Cielle twirled the phone cord around her wrist and waited.

"I could lose my job," the operator said.

Cielle shut her eyes. The operator cleared her throat.

"I've taken an oath," she said.

The Amish women brought in more food and then ushered the children outside when they saw her on the phone. Cielle watched them leave. They spoke a language she'd not heard before, a variation of the German she'd heard on the radio. They were harsh, angular, throaty words. Yet she knew from the women's tone and gestures they were telling the girls it was rude to be in the house and to get outside. Cielle watched their bunned hair and bonnets as they scurried into the yard and drive, and beyond she caught sight of her mother and John standing behind a buggy.

"If it was your father," Cielle said.

Cielle heard a clicking noise and turned. Hannah was still there, fooling with the light in the living room, listening.

"Of course," the operator said.

"Wouldn't you want to know why your father died?"

Hannah looked at Cielle and didn't take her eyes off her.

"Okay, hang up," Helen said. "Now." The operator sniffled on the other end. Cielle's palm sweated on the phone.

Helen grabbed the butt of the phone and pulled. Cielle's grip tightened.

"Hang up." Helen yanked the phone from her. "Enough of this." The phone slipped from Cielle's hand and Helen set it back in its cradle.

Hannah stopped flipping the light switch.

"There's no secret answer, Cielle. There's nothing that will make this anything but what it is," Helen said.

"You don't know."

"Yes, I do."

"You're scared to know."

"No." Helen shook her head back and forth. "I'm not."

"You don't want to know reasons. Because they'll change you."

"Haven't our lives changed enough already?"

They stood face-to-face, eye-to-eye. Neither flinched. Cielle breathed through her nose; her nostrils flared.

"And do the reasons even matter? I'm going outside to help," Helen said. "And you should too. Both of you. Let this go, Cielle." She turned and walked out the door.

Cielle looked at Hannah and picked up the phone again. She put her finger over her lips. "Don't say anything." Hannah nodded yes.

The operator came on the line. "Hello, Miss Cielle."

"The Olsen house, please."

The line rang. Mr. Olsen answered.

"Your wife knows something and she needs to tell me," Cielle said.

"Who the hell is this?"

"Cielle Jacobson."

"You don't know what you're talking

about, young lady."

"I know more than you do."

"You don't know anything."

"What happened between her and my father? Why is she afraid to talk about it?"

"What are you accusing her of, exactly?"

"I'm not sure yet."

"You have some nerve." He snorted and hung up the phone.

"You have some nerve," she said to the empty line, and hung up.

Hannah touched Cielle's arm. "My father died too," she said. "He was needed elsewhere," she said. She believed it, and seemed at peace with it. Peace like a river, peace like quiet in the woods with nothing but leaves moving above, peace like a field of purple clover in sundown light.

That belief in God's will and faith that things happened for a reason was something Cielle had never had. What if she'd been thinking wrong? What were the possibilities of a God in all that was unseen, unknown, and unknowable? What if her father dying was part of something larger, like those stars in the night sky? And even if there wasn't a God to believe in, what if there was a force in the universe that had everyone's stories mapped out?

■ ■ ■ ■

The Amish men were practiced — they moved about one another gracefully, and knew where to go and what to do. Every man had a job. They raised wall frames with rope and hammered them together. The body of the barn stood sturdy by noon. Post and beam. Solid pine. A beautiful skeleton of wood with strong lines intersecting. Something new on top of something old. The old foundation was good, they said. It didn't need any fixing. It could hold anything they put on top of it.

At noon, one man blew a whistle and all the men and women and children stopped. They gathered in a circle and everyone fell silent.

"What happened?" Cielle asked.

"They're saying the Lord's Prayer before lunch," her mother said.

Heads bowed. They formed a chain and every single person held someone else's hand. A sea of dark bodies, white bonnets, and straw hats like halos. Angels. Her mother held her hand. Cielle said the prayer to herself, in her own head, to see if she could remember it. *Our father, who art in heaven, hallowed be thy name. Thy kingdom come, thy will be done, on earth as it is in heaven. Give us this day our daily bread. And forgive us our debts, as we forgive our debtors. And lead us not into temptation, but deliver us from evil: for thine is the kingdom and the power and the glory, forever. Amen.*

The Amish broke the chain and went to the kitchen for the food that had been brought. Some sat under trees, and some sat in the field on the grass that had been cut but hadn't been baled, where pieces of her father's note still lay scattered. Cielle, her mother, her grandmother, and Helen walked around with pitchers of water, filling up tin cups the Amish had brought from home. Each person thanked Cielle for the water and she thanked them for the barn. Despite their clothes that made them look different, Cielle saw they were mothers, fathers, sons, and daughters. They were families.

She wandered and watched people. Suspenders, lace-up boots, women's hair parted down the middle and smoothed back into buns, long beards with the mustache shaved on older men. Wet, dark patches of sweat on shirts and shining sweat on the backs of necks and foreheads. Yet no one complained, and no one spoke about the heat or being tired of the war. She felt immodest in her

224

sundress. Young men and women watched her with curious eyes and Cielle wondered if it was envy or judgment.

"Cielle, why don't you sit and lunch here with me?" John sat fifty feet in front of her and patted the ground next to him. She walked in his direction and extended the pitcher of water to his cup. He nodded in thanks, took off his straw hat, and set it on the ground beside him.

"I should get more water."

"You can sit," he said. "You need to eat too. I have extra."

She didn't want to be rude, so she sat and righted the pitcher on a groove in the grass so it wouldn't tip. He was younger than she had first thought. He didn't yet have lines on his face, and his hands weren't aged the way her father's hands had been, with freckled and weathered, ridged skin. Bright white half-moons rounded from the cuticles on his fingernails. Her father had had them too, and he'd said they were a sign of health. She'd wanted them on her own fingers, but only ever had them faintly on her thumbs like small faded hills.

He noticed her gaze and held up his hand. "Rising moons," he said. "Mine are extra-big. It's a sign of health."

Cielle scratched her nose and nodded. He

handed her half a ham sandwich on thick, dark bread.

"How old are you?" she asked.

"Twenty-five," he said.

"I've seen you before," she said.

"At the farmers' market and the viewing," he said. He wiped his mouth on his handkerchief. "Your father was a good man. He'll be missed."

"Do I know you from something else?"

"No," he said, and bent his knee up toward his chest and tied his bootlace. "I think there was no time but now when we were supposed to know each other. One thing ends and another begins. This is one of those instances."

Behind John's shoulder, Cielle saw her mother and grandmother surveying the group, each holding a water pitcher in front of her like a shield. Then her mother spotted Cielle and made to walk in her direction but her grandmother held her back by the shoulder. John turned to look where Cielle was looking.

"Who will watch after your mother?"

"She'll watch after herself."

He nodded.

"She expects us to leave, you know. We're expected to have a separate life."

"I know," he said. "We're expected to stay

and care for one another."

"That's good you have people all around you, no matter what."

"We all need looking after." He ate the last of his sandwich and crumpled the waxed paper into a ball. "I'll be checking in on you and your mother."

He looked at Cielle and ran his hands through his dark blond hair. His eyes were light blue. He was so familiar. He took a bite of his sandwich and nodded at the barn. "This will be a good structure. This will last you hundreds of years."

"You know, Old Mr. Olsen will likely keep this land. So this barn will be for him."

"He won't be keeping this land."

She picked at the grass.

The whistle blew. John drank the rest of his water. He knelt on one knee and dusted off his hat. He stood, settled his hat onto his head, and tied his tool belt around his waist. He held out his hand for Cielle. She took his hand and he pulled her up.

"My father and I have worked something out with your mother," John said. "We're going to farm your land, and you stay in the house."

"I don't understand."

"There's nothing to understand, Cielle, except that this is going to be a beautiful,

beautiful barn."

She walked to the house with her empty pitcher. Her mother stood by the door. "They put these barns up fast, don't they?" Her mother leaned over and adjusted the strap of Cielle's dress — she untwisted it and straightened it on her shoulder. With both hands she turned Cielle's head away from her and took out the elastic in her hair, smoothed her hair down, and ran her fingers over her scalp and neck like a comb. Cielle's head tingled and her face relaxed. Her mother hadn't fixed her hair in weeks. Cielle eased her shoulders and shut her eyes as her mother's fingers combed around her temples and ears and the base of her hairline, and gathered her hair back into a neat ponytail.

Her mother patted her head to let her know she was finished. Cielle turned back. Her mother looked ahead, as if she were able to put the barn together by the sheer will of envisioning it finished. The hammering began again. There was the lifting and shifting of boards, and the scrape and zip of saws ripping through wood.

"I like him," Cielle said.

Her mother nodded yes.

"He reminds me of Dad," Cielle said.

"I know it." Her mother smiled.

In a corner of the living room, Cielle assembled her father's belongings: his black-scuffed work boots that smelled of leather and polish, his straw hat, his green coffee mug, his razor, his farming journal with his angular handwriting. How could she save her father's words, knowledge, and comfort that the world was a good place, but also a place where things would happen that you never expected to happen? How could she save her father's smell of fresh soap on pillowcases, the stubble-itch of a kiss on the cheek, his blue eyes that were Helen's eyes, and his birdcall?

She'd miss their walks through the sun-dappled woods looking for hidden treasures like arrowheads and archaeological remains. *Maybe we'll discover another Boaz mastodon,* he'd say. *Look hard, look closely for bones, for any sign of life once lived.* They had talked about finding a species no one ever knew existed before and made up possibilities: winged stallions, giant pigs, purple-feathered birds that could breathe underwater, alligators with emerald eyes, and bluebirds with feathers made of silk and bones of silver and gold. *It's been said the bluebird carries the blue of heaven on his back and the rich brown of the freshly turned earth on his breast,* he had said as they walked past wild wood sorrel, scarlet trumpet honeysuckle, and wood and maidenhair ferns, looking for lives before their own, looking for clues about how life was lived and to how to live their lives. She took his things and placed them in a box. She'd put them away, safe, for the memory of his life lived. She set the box in her bedroom. She'd carry it for the rest of her life.

The Olsens' fancy Cadillac pulled into the driveway. They drove right up as if they deserved to, were important, and knew her family well. She knew it wasn't to help build the barn. Mr. Olsen swung out of the car with a fury in his eyes. His face was red, as if he'd held his breath on the drive over. Mrs. Olsen followed him, her eyes on the backs of his knees as he walked toward the door. Cielle went downstairs and outside.

"Who's in charge of Cielle?" he asked.

"She's mine." Her mother stepped forward and stood in front of him.

"It ends today." He pointed a finger at the ground. "Right now."

"If this is about your father and the land . . ." her mother said.

Some people stopped working to listen, but mostly the building and hammering continued. Darren put down his hammer and took off his gloves. Mr. Olsen scanned the property and pointed at Darren. "You. Get over here." But Darren didn't move. When Mr. Olsen's eyes found Cielle, he pointed at her. "And you. I've had enough of you."

"I've had enough of you," Cielle said.

"You little bitch," he said, and balled his fists.

Darren moved toward his father, but Cielle's mother stepped in front of him and stood between Darren and his father. "You are on my property and the way you're speaking to my daughter is ticking me off."

"You don't know what she's done."

"I'm sure it would make me proud."

"She blamed my wife for your husband's death."

"Why would she do that?" her mother asked.

"I didn't say that," Cielle said.

"You implied it," Mr. Olsen said.

"She should have known something was wrong," Cielle said.

"No," Mrs. Olsen said. "I couldn't have known."

Her mother stepped closer to Mrs. Olsen. "Look at me." She snapped her fingers. Mrs. Olsen looked her in the eye. "Why should you have known?"

"He came to me for help."

"He what?"

"Counseling."

"How long?"

"Six months."

Cielle's mother looked beyond Mrs. Olsen, but remained standing close to her. "You see what's going on here?" her mother asked. She was so close to Mrs. Olsen she could have kissed her. Mrs. Olsen did not budge. "There's a new barn going up where the tornado took the old one down."

"I see that," Mrs. Olsen said.

"And here's me and my girls." She fixed her eyes back on Mrs. Olsen. "Lee's supposed to be here but he's not."

Tears fell down Mrs. Olsen's cheeks. "I didn't know this would happen."

"I've got a fifteen-year-old trying to make sense of her father's death. What she doesn't understand yet, because she's a girl even though she thinks she's a full woman, is that for some things there is no sense."

Mrs. Olsen nodded in agreement. "I know."

"I know you know that, because you're a mother. Do you understand that, Mr. Olsen?" He stood with his arms crossed and looked at the sky and puckered his lips.

"I have a fifteen-year-old girl trying to figure out her daddy's dying," Cielle's mother said. "Do you hear me?"

"We all have our struggles," Mr. Olsen said. "We'll leave you to yours if you leave us to ours."

"All right?" her mother asked Cielle.

"Yes, Mother," Cielle said.

"We all have our own hurt to carry," her mother said.

"Come on, Darren," Mr. Olsen said. "Get in the car."

"I'm not going anywhere," Darren said. "I'm staying right here and building this barn."

And at that his parents turned and left.

The construction continued through the evening. The barn was finished in three days. On the fourth day it was painted red, and it was beautiful. Cielle requested an outside barn light in the same place as the last one, so she could find her way home in the dark.

CHAPTER THIRTEEN

Cielle and her father had a collection of arrowheads they'd found near Mill Creek. Most were made out of plain rock, and a few made of smoky quartz or black obsidian. They'd found eleven altogether. Her father kept them in an old blue tobacco tin on a shelf in the cellar. She brought the tin upstairs, rinsed the arrowheads off in the kitchen sink, and laid them out on a towel. Her father's favorite was the black obsidian arrowhead with smooth, shiny grooves leading toward its sharp point. She kept that one for herself.

She divvied up some of the others to give away to her mother, Helen, her grandmother, Mr. and Mrs. Mitchell, Bodie, and Darren. She would bury the rest in the garden, and put them back in the earth from where they had come, treasures of an old world for others to find.

Some thought taking arrowheads was bad

luck, but her father had said he believed things were left behind to be found. That what we found was left so we could understand and remember. "Arrowheads are good luck," he said. "They point us in the right direction and protect us."

Direction and protection were things she thought they could all use.

It was a Monday, the twenty-third of August. She chose a quartz arrowhead for Bodie. She wrapped it in a cotton handkerchief that had belonged to her father. Cielle, her mother, and Helen drove to the train station and waited on the platform. When Bodie and his parents arrived, Bodie had nothing but a duffel bag and the clothes on his back. Cielle did not want to say goodbye, but it was better than saying nothing.

Bodie dropped the bag at his feet. Mrs. Mitchell stood behind him and put her hands on his shoulders, squeezed, and didn't let go.

"Train takes three full days to San Antonio," Mrs. Mitchell said.

"Long," Cielle said.

"He'll get to see some of this great country," Mr. Mitchell said. "Forest, plains, mountains, and desert."

Cielle's mother went to hug Bodie. "Be safe," she said. "Come home."

Cielle felt her cheeks get hot. The train's engine began with a loud chug and sputter.

Bodie fluttered his hands at Cielle. "Come on," he said, "come here." He opened his arms.

She practically tripped into him, and put her head against his chest and her arms around his waist. He was so warm; she felt his chest rise and fall. His arms were tight around her. Then he squeezed three times.

"I love you," he said, and kissed the top of her head. She looked at him and he looked at her, and she knew she'd always love him, no matter where he went or what happened.

She held out the handkerchief. "It's an arrowhead. It's for direction and safety."

He put it in his breast pocket and patted it. "Thank you."

There were other families on the platform saying their good-byes, sending sons off to war, taking good looks for what might be the last time. Cielle thought, You never know if you'll see someone again. You never know how your life might change in an instant. You don't know how you'll miss them until they're gone. She could imagine the missing if it was anything like missing her father. It was a missing that couldn't be filled. It was a space like an empty piece of sky that followed her around.

Helen and Bodie held on to each other, exchanged words she couldn't hear, and kissed and cried. When they pulled apart, Bodie kissed Helen's hand and she touched the side of his face with an open palm. Then she walked straight toward the parking lot and didn't look back, and Cielle knew it was because she couldn't look back and Bodie didn't want her to. And then Bodie was on the train and the train was gone, and this person she'd known her whole life was gone. And she knew again that the world was full of things she'd never know or be able to understand.

The three of them drove home without saying a word.

One week later they unloaded Helen's car in Madison. The dorm room was a tiny double with a twin bed against each wall and dressers at the foot of the beds. Helen's roommate was a girl from Milwaukee named Clara. She wore a string of pearls, had perfect teeth straight and white as a picket fence, and kept saying, *I'm so happy to meet you, I'm so excited to be here. Can you believe it?*

"I can," Helen said more than once. "I can believe it."

"Is that your car out there?" Clara pointed

down below out the window.

"It is," Helen said.

"That's some car. You know how to drive it?"

"Where we live, you can't get far unless you drive."

"I can't drive."

Cielle's mother looked at Cielle and widened her eyes as she took clothes out of Helen's suitcase and neatly folded them into dresser drawers.

"My daddy thinks ladies don't drive," Clara said, and fingered her pearls, one by one, then put her necklace in her mouth and rolled it between her lips.

"My father gave me that car," Helen said, and walked to the window next to Clara and leaned over to look down.

"It's a great car," Cielle said, and admired its shiny sloping hood and bright hubcaps. "I can drive too."

"I took the train here, by myself. My parents had an event to attend," Clara said.

"So ladies can take trains by themselves but they can't drive?" Helen asked.

"I guess so," Clara said. She reached for her purse, opened the window, and lit a cigarette.

"And they smoke?" Cielle asked.

"When they're out of their father's watchful eye, they do. Will you teach me how to drive?" Clara asked.

"Sure," Helen said.

Cielle unpacked one of Helen's paintings and hung it on a hook over her bed.

"Your farm?" Clara asked.

"Something like it," Helen said.

"That looks like our new barn," Cielle said.

Cielle's mother stepped closer to look at the painting. She flung one of Helen's dresses over her shoulder and crossed her arms. "It does look like our new barn."

"I painted that a year ago," Helen said.

"Maybe you had a vision of what was to come," her mother said.

The painting, of the red barn set in green grass with a blue sky, was how Cielle wanted to remember their barn over time, as if that had always been their barn: a dreamy dot of red in a sea of rich vegetation. Vibrant. Intact. A beating heart. A swell of love in the middle of nowhere. An arrow that pointed to a red dot that marked the spot of home. *You are here. This is where you belong.*

Helen stood on the train platform in her white eyelet dress, her blond hair falling over her shoulders. Helen wore the same dress she wore the day Cielle walked into the barn and found their father. The same dress that moved toward Cielle six weeks ago now stood still as Cielle moved away on the train. Helen was such a pretty girl. Cielle wondered if she'd always recognize her sister if she saw her on a platform, or in a crowded station. She wondered when she'd see Helen next and if she'd be different. If she'd smoke cigarettes, wear pearls, swim at night in Lake Mendota, be dating Matthew, know more about the physics of time and space, loneliness and love. The train moved slowly out of the station and rumbled over the tracks.

Helen waved. Cielle opened the window, stuck her head out, and waved back. Helen blew kisses and Cielle blew them back. Her eyes filled with tears and everything blurred. The train gained speed and Cielle's hair whipped in her face. Helen became smaller and smaller. Her white dress a ghost, a distant cloud, a snowflake, and then the train curved around a bend and she was gone.

Cielle and her mother rode the train from Madison back to Richland Center. Some train cars had old wicker seats, open windows for air, and were filled with soldiers on the move and sometimes drunk. She couldn't blame them. Every young man seemed to have joined the forces.

In Boaz, their grandmother would be gone, back to her own life. Bodie was gone to places she couldn't imagine. He would be one of the soldiers in uniform, one of so many men putting their lives on the line for strangers, leaving their families at the risk of never coming home again.

Cielle already missed what was gone of her childhood, and what was leaving little by little every day. She already missed her years at home with the soft living and loving words. She missed all that was and would be left unsaid. When things changed, they were never the same again. And they kept changing. They never stopped changing.

The swamp maples were beginning to turn — their red leaves flashed here and there as the world sped by. She kept the window open, and the late afternoon air smelled thinner, cooler, and papery. The smells marked the end of summer and the coming of autumn. Life into death into life, again and again and again.

She envisioned mastodons — brown woolly beasts moving slowly through the hills and fields, or lying about just as common as the cows and horses of the present day. She thought about how, back then or even now, no one imagined a whole species could become extinct. Maybe no one understood disappearance, but only knew its acute ache — the ache of missing, memory, and mystery that maybe dulls over time or maybe doesn't.

The train hurled toward the bruise of night. Wheels spun. It was the sound of, *Shush shush shhhhhhhhh, be quiet, don't say a word.* It was the sound of, *Hush. Hush, little darling, don't you cry.* It was the sound of something sliding out of reach, the sound of their lives passing by. She felt a longing deep inside. A need to search for something, someplace, someone. There were so many things yet to know, and so much she would never know. Could never know. *People survive all sorts of things,* Cielle thought, *and love is one of them. There is no simple straight answer in life. There is no single cause for anything. People survive all sorts of things,* she thought, *and loss is one of them.*

As fields and farmland passed outside, a definitive line separated sky from land, separated blue from green, yellow, tan, and brown. It was the horizon line, and it seemed within reach, that narrow space where day begins and ends, that separation between heaven and earth.

ACKNOWLEDGMENTS

The first chapter of this novel originally appeared in a slightly different form as a short story in *The Iowa Review,* and was awarded the 2005 Iowa Review Prize; I'm grateful to Chris Offutt for choosing my story that year.

With thanks to the Kenyon Review Writers Workshop and Bread Loaf Writers' Conference, and the Tickner Writing Fellowship for time and support; to Crystal Foley at the Richland Center Historical Room at the Brewer Public Library, and to Don Goplin and Mike Jacobson for help with research on the region and time period; to Heather Dermott for reading early pages; to Alyssum Wier for always listening; to Jenniffer Gray and Alvaro Salcedo for being constant and true; to my dear friends who know who they are; and to my writing communities near and far, for support and inspiration.

To PJ Mark, for believing in this novel first.

To Starling Lawrence, for saying yes, and for his smart and generous editing and guidance.

With appreciation for the team at W. W. Norton, for their care and hard work in making beautiful books.

Thank you to my family, particularly my mother, for traveling back to Boaz with me; to my father, for being my trusted reader, and a champion of my writing; to my sister; to the Jacobsons, Bredahls, and Calverts; and to my grandmother, who was known as Jake, who was loved by all, who made the best pies, and from whom we all learned kindness, strength, and resilience.

ABOUT THE AUTHOR

Meghan Kenny is the author of *Love Is No Small Thing: Stories.* Her short story "The Driest Season" — the basis for her debut novel — won the Iowa Review Award and was a Pushcart Prize Special Mention. She lives in Lancaster, Pennsylvania.